Praise for V. M. Burns and her Mys

KILLER WOR

"Charming. . . . Newcomers will have fun, while established fans will relish the evolution of the characters and welcome Samantha's bright new future." —*Publishers Weekly*

A TOURIST'S GUIDE TO MURDER

"Colorful characters and just enough mystery trivia boost the fast-moving plot. Cozy fans are sure to have fun." —*Publishers Weekly*

BOOKMARKED FOR MURDER

"This two-in-one mystery satisfies on so many levels, with this fifth in the series being as fresh and unique as the first." —*Kings River Life* magazine

"In the end, *Bookmarked for Murder* is a fantastic bookstore cozy murder book, and the 'Mystery Bookshop' series is an enthralling read that makes me smile and has me hoping my retirement will be just like Nana Jo's and the other characters'. This book is beyond entertaining. It's a page-turner that is filled with remarkable characters that have readers coming back for more." —*The Cozy Review*

READ HERRING HUNT

"As good as any Jessica Fletcher story could be, Burns has a way with words and her characters are absolutely riveting. There is no doubt this is one series that will continue for a good, long time to come." —*Suspense* magazine

THE PLOT IS MURDER

"This debut cleverly integrates a historical cozy within a contemporary mystery. In both story lines, the elder characters shine; they are refreshingly witty and robust, with formidable connections and investigative skills." —*Library Journal* (starred review)

Books by Valerie Burns

Baker Street Mysteries
TWO PARTS SUGAR, ONE PART MURDER

Books by Valerie Burns writing as V. M. Burns

Mystery Bookshop Mysteries
THE PLOT IS MURDER
READ HERRING HUNT
THE NOVEL ART OF MURDER
WED, READ & DEAD
BOOKMARKED FOR MURDER
A TOURIST'S GUIDE TO MURDER
KILLER WORDS
BOOKCLUBBED TO DEATH

Dog Club Mysteries
IN THE DOG HOUSE
THE PUPPY WHO KNEW TOO MUCH
BARK IF IT'S MURDER
PAW AND ORDER
SIT, STAY, SLAY

Published by Kensington Publishing Corp.

Bookclubbed to Death

V. M. BURNS

KENSINGTON
PUBLISHING CORP.
www.kensingtonbooks.com

This book is dedicated to Col. Sandy Edge.
Thank you for your service.

Chapter 1

"Snickers, come!" I yelled. My hands were shaking so badly that I fumbled to unlock Oreo's crate. Eventually, I got the lock open, turned, and hurried out of the room, confident that the dog who trailed me around the house like a shadow would follow. I was halfway across the living room before I realized I was alone.

The wind roared as the rain pounded against the windows.

I hurried back to my bedroom. Snickers was still curled up in the center of my bed, oblivious to the storm raging outside. "Snickers." I shook her.

Fourteen, with more white around her muzzle than brown, my barely eight-pound toy poodle lifted her head and yawned. Her breath halted me for a split second before I held my own, reached over and scooped her up, and looked around for Oreo.

"Samantha Marie Washington, what is taking you so long?" Nana Jo said. "We need to get down in the basement now."

"I can't find Oreo." I frantically scanned my bedroom, looking to see what could have happened to him. "I just had him. I had to come back for Snickers, and he got away from me."

Oreo, my male toy poodle, would normally have bounced out of his crate. Always energetic, Oreo was still more a puppy than his twelve years showed.

A tiny brown head poked out from underneath the bed and glanced around before sliding back underneath.

"He's terrified. Here." I handed Snickers to Nana Jo and got down on my knees.

"We don't have time for this, Dorothy. That tornado is almost on top of us, and I left my magic wand and shiny red shoes at the dry cleaners." Before I could comment on *The Wizard of Oz* reference, Nana Jo pushed her flashlight in my hand. "Oreo, come here right now." She turned and walked out of the room.

A few seconds later, there was a loud boom of lightning, and the lights flashed.

Oreo stuck out his head from underneath the bed and then flew after Nana Jo, leaving me on my knees.

Another loud crack, and I hurried after them.

The power went out just as I started down the stairs from my apartment to the bookstore on the first floor. I turned to the right and headed toward my office. There was a coat closet, but Nana Jo had already removed my rain slicker and boots and left them out and ready for me.

I shoved my feet down in the pink rubber boots my grandmother called galoshes. My rain slicker was yellow and was an exact replica of one I'd had as a kid with metal clasps and a hood. I pushed my arms through the slicker. I yanked open the door and held on for a few seconds while the winds pummeled me. I pulled the door closed and braced myself as I pushed against the winds and made my way the few short steps to the cellar door.

One of the only things I disliked about the building,

which was now my business and my home, was that the only way to reach the basement was from outside. The entrance to the cellar was on an angled and raised platform and formed a triangle slanting down from about three feet up the side of the building to the ground. We usually kept a padlock on the doors, but Nana Jo had already taken care of that. Concrete stairs led underground. It was dark, damp, with an earthy smell that reminded me of worms and other creepy-crawly things that slithered on the ground. I hated dark basements.

The wind wrenched the door out of my hand, and I had to use all of my strength to pull it closed.

I followed a dim shaft of light to the bottom, where I found Nana Jo dripping water from the hood of her slicker with two poodles clutched to her chest. "It's not often that tornadoes actually touch down this close to Lake Michigan, but we'll be safe here," she said. Her voice sounded confident, but there was a flash of unease behind her eyes, which was the only sign that she was as nervous as I was.

Tornadoes were a hazard of living in the Midwest, and I remember going through drills in elementary school and during the years when I taught English in the high school before I quit to open a mystery bookshop. However, even with decades of practice, I couldn't recall a tornado actually touching down.

"I'm glad Dawson's away at football camp," I said with as much conviction as I could muster up. Even to my own ears, my words didn't sound convincing. My assistant, Dawson Alexander, was a quarterback for Michigan Southwest University, or what the locals called Miss You. He was over six feet tall and two hundred pounds of pure muscle. In my head, I knew there wasn't much he could do to keep us safe from forces of nature, but I think his bulky presence would have helped my emotional state.

"Sam, come here and sit down." Nana Jo patted a spot on

the workbench, which was under the chimney. She pulled Oreo out from inside her coat and attempted to hand him to me. However, his claws gripped her sweater, and it took both of us to pry that ten-pound poodle off. At five foot ten and two hundred pounds, Nana Jo was no lightweight.

Once freed from the warmth and safety of Nana Jo, Oreo leaped onto my chest, clasped my neck, and held on for dear life. I held his shivering body close and whispered soothing words of nonsense to comfort him.

The rain crashed against the metal doors of the cellar, but the old brick brownstone was steady and strong. The storm raged outside, and at one point, Oreo lifted his head and howled, something I'd never heard him do before. However, after a few moments, the tempest subsided. When the wind was barely more than a bluster, Nana Jo walked up the steps and listened for a few seconds before opening the door.

Outside, the night was eerily quiet. The moon glowed and cast a yellow beam of light through the night sky that mixed with the darkness to form a purplish haze.

Nana Jo climbed up and out, with Snickers still wrapped tightly inside her raincoat.

Oreo and I followed.

Once out of the dank-smelling basement, the air had a fishy smell that felt heavy and close.

"That certainly was an adventure." I looked around to survey the damage done by the storm. Apart from leaves, branches, and a few pieces of debris that floated through our yard, all was well.

I glanced down at my phone and wasn't surprised to see that I didn't have cell service. Given the force of those winds, it would have been surprising if I did. I prayed my family were all well and walked around to the front to look at the street.

Everything that wasn't bolted to the ground was rolling around the street. Garbage and recycle bins, patio furniture, trash, and a mangled piece of metal that had once been a bicycle. Thankfully, the shops that lined Market Street appeared to have only sustained minor damage. All of the front windows were spared, and nothing more significant than a few tree limbs had landed on the property. I walked the short distance to North Harbor Café, the restaurant owned by my fiancé, Frank Patterson, and let out a sigh of relief. His restaurant was unharmed. I pulled out my phone to send him a text before I remembered that I didn't have cell service.

"What did we do before cell phones?" I asked.

Nana Jo shrugged. "Wrote letters, sent telegrams, and if we were really desperate, we actually talked face-to-face after we finished beating our clothes with rocks at the river."

"Very funny. You know what I mean."

She grinned. "I do know what you mean. Modern conveniences have made our lives a lot easier. When they work, they're fantastic."

"When they don't, it reminds us how much we rely on technology."

"They'll have it back on soon."

"Let's drive by Jenna's, and then we can drive out to Shady Acres." I turned to walk around the building and headed toward the garage.

Nana Jo cleared her throat. "Sam, don't you think you should put on some clothes first?"

I glanced down. I was still wearing galoshes and the raincoat I'd grabbed earlier on top of the long T-shirt that I slept in. I didn't need a mirror to see that my face was red. I could feel the heat as it moved up my neck.

I clutched the jacket and hurried upstairs to change into outside clothes. I pretended not to notice my grandmother laughing.

It didn't take long to change. The longest part was extracting Oreo, who had his claws in my nightshirt and refused to let go. The poor little guy was shivering and determined. Snickers curled up in the center of the bed and waited. Once I had on pants and a sweatshirt, I scooped up both poodles and hurried out.

I handed Snickers to Nana Jo and got behind the wheel. Once I was seated, she helped me extract Oreo, who quickly latched onto her.

Nana Jo reached into her purse and pulled out a small glass bottle. She unscrewed the lid, which was a dropper. I watched as she filled the dropper and then squirted it in Oreo's muzzle. "Good thing you had some of that CBD oil left over from the Fourth of July."

"I was wondering if we had any more of that stuff. It worked wonders to settle the poor guy down after the fireworks." I pushed the button to raise the garage door, put the car in reverse, and pulled out.

"I'm not sure if it's the oil or the bacon flavoring, but he loves this stuff, and it sure helps reduce his anxiety."

Not to be left out, Snickers scratched at Nana Jo's arm until she gave her a smaller dose of the oil. Oreo held on to Nana Jo's shoulder, but his shivering lessened. Snickers made two small circles in Nana Jo's lap and then curled into a ball and went to sleep.

Most of the damage to North Harbor that we saw involved fallen tree limbs. However, a few of the branches had fallen on power lines that forced us to take detours. The drive from my store to my sister Jenna's house shouldn't have taken more than fifteen minutes. However, nearly forty minutes later, I pulled in front of my sister's Victorian home.

Despite its location on the shores of Lake Michigan, where lakefront property typically garnered big bucks, North Harbor was still recovering from the race riots of the sixties and the manufacturing exodus of the late seventies and early eighties. With both the St. Thomas River and Lake Michigan as lures, North Harbor had all of the ingredients to attract tourists, as did its twin city of South Harbor. Sharing the same Lake Michigan shoreline, North and South Harbor, Michigan, were identical in that respect but exact opposites in practically everything else. South Harbor had a thriving economy fueled by the tourists who traveled near and far to walk its cobblestoned streets, tour lighthouses, or play on the sandy beaches. Cross the St. Thomas River into North Harbor, and the downtown was full of old, boarded-up brick buildings that had been allowed to decay and crumble from years of neglect. Diehard residents with long memories of the days when manufacturing plants that supported the Motor City brought high-paying jobs to town worked to rebuild the economy. That was one of the reasons that my late husband, Leon, and I wanted to open our mystery bookshop in North Harbor. We dreamed of quitting our mundane jobs and indulging in our passion.

The city's historic district was a perfect reflection of the area's once regal history. From its days as home to a religion known as the House of David, to the home of manufacturing tycoons who supported the state's automotive industry, North Harbor's historic district held grand old Victorian and Georgian homes, cobblestoned streets, and yards enclosed by wrought-iron fences. When the manufacturing companies fled the city, many of the houses fell into disrepair. Those that remained were either converted into rentals or left to decay. In one of the waves of economic renovation that hit the area, the city bought many of the derelict homes and sold them for one dollar to individuals willing to rehab and live in them versus renting. My sister and her husband, Tony, were among the first to buy and had spent the last quarter of a century turning what my father used to refer to as their "money pit" into their dream home.

I breathed a sigh of relief when I saw the large oak trees

that shaded their home were still there, albeit minus a few limbs that had abandoned their trunks but thankfully had fallen on the ground rather than the house.

"Thank God they're safe, and the twins are at school," Nana Jo said.

Jenna and Tony were standing on the porch with two suitcases when we arrived.

My sister was four years older than me, but you couldn't tell it by looking at her. We were both about the same height, five foot four, but I'm pretty sure I had about twenty pounds on her . . . maybe thirty. Although my sister kept her hair short and immaculately coiffed, we both had brown eyes and brown hair. I was doing better at taking care of my hair since my sister had staged an intervention and introduced me to her stylist.

I pointed at the suitcases. "Going somewhere?"

"No power," Jenna said. "We've been trying to find a hotel in the area, but they're filling up fast."

I stopped. "Wait, you have cell service?"

She shook her head. "We never took out our landline. Zaq and Christopher called to check on us. Zaq's been checking the Internet and relaying the information back."

Zaq and Christopher were my nephews. Recently graduated from Jesus and Mary University or JAMU in nearby River Bend, Indiana, they both secured jobs at a technology company in Chicago and moved to set up their apartment. The boys were twins, but they were also very different. Christopher would be working in marketing, while Zaq was going to be doing something with information technology, which I couldn't explain if my life depended on it.

"We were going to wait it out, but according to Zaq, the electric company isn't expecting our power to be on for a couple of days." Jenna turned to me. "What about you? Is your power on?"

"It's on now. Yes. You don't have to waste money finding a hotel. You're welcome to stay with me."

"Or you can stay at my house," Nana Jo said. "The power rarely goes out at Shady Acres."

After my grandfather died, Nana Jo sold their home and bought a new home in a senior retirement community built on Lake Michigan's shoreline. The area included single-family homes referred to as villas, town houses, and a building full of condominiums and apartments.

Jenna laughed. "Why no power outages at the retirement village? Too many old folks with pacemakers?"

Shady Acres was a community for active seniors with everything from tennis, golf, martial arts, painting, and a host of other activities.

Nana Jo feigned shock and swatted Jenna's bottom. "Too many gamers who get ticked off if their games drop or folks streaming videos who'll drop-kick you if they miss an episode of *Pick My Mate*."

"Ugh. I can't believe anyone watches that show." Jenna stared at Nana Jo and narrowed her gaze. "Don't tell me you watch that stupidity."

"Don't be daft. Of course not. I'd rather gouge my eyes out with a dull spoon than watch a show where someone allows millions of strangers to choose the person they should go on a date with as though they were ordering pizza."

I snickered.

"There's also Mom's place," I said. "Since she and Harold moved to Australia, they certainly won't be needing it."

"Are you joking? There's no way I'd move back there even for a day." My sister, the lawyer, must have felt the objection coming up and smacked it down before the words even left my mouth. "Once I was old enough to move out of that plastic paradise, I vowed never again."

I couldn't joke because I'd made the same vow. My mother had encased the house in plastic to prevent two daughters who were more tomboy than debutante from bringing even a speck of dust into her home. Plastic runners provided a walking path that ran from the front door to the back door and every hallway and stair in between. She'd even had custom slipcovers made from plastic for all of the upholstered furniture. To this day, the sound of tape being ripped from a box sends shivers up my spine and memories of my flesh being ripped from my legs during hot summer months.

"Do you think Harold will let Mom plasticize their new house?" I joked.

"He's probably already bought all of the plastic in the country," Nana Jo said. "That man worships the ground your mother walks on."

My mom's new husband, Harold Robertson, was rich. His family had owned one of the most prominent department stores in the area when I was a kid. Even though Harold hadn't followed the family path and gone into retail, he'd followed his heart and become an aeronautical engineer with NASA. He was a nice man whose only fault was that he worshipped my mother, and his generosity knew no bounds, which is why he was now living in Sydney with my mom on an adventure to save the koala bear.

"Are you kidding?" I chuckled. "I'm guessing he's cornered the plastic runner and furniture market."

When we stopped laughing, Nana Jo shoved a set of keys into my sister's hands.

"Water my plants while you're there," Nana Jo said.

Frank Patterson pulled up, and I heaved a sigh of relief.

"Glad you're here," Nana Jo said. "Now Sam can stop looking at her watch every two minutes."

I ignored my grandmother and gave my fiancé a big hug. "We were headed by your place next. I just—"

He stopped me with a kiss. "You don't need to apologize to me for making sure your family is safe."

I returned his kiss. "You're a part of my family, too."

He whispered a few words that made me blush and then held my hand while we walked up onto the porch so he could greet the rest of the family.

Frank Patterson was tall with salt-and-pepper hair, soft brown eyes, and a big smile. A few years ago, he'd retired from the military and moved to North Harbor to follow his dream of opening a restaurant. After my late husband, Leon, died, my heart broke into a million pieces. I never dreamed that I could put it together again, but then Frank bought the building a few doors down from my bookstore. He was kind, generous, and supportive, and I learned that my heart wasn't as brittle as I had once thought. Frank's past was still a mystery. He'd spent years in government agencies that he wasn't at liberty to discuss. However, since we started planning to get married, he'd started to share more of his personal past, including the fact that his mother was still alive and couldn't wait to meet me. Now, that was terrifying. I'd had an excellent relationship with my last mother-in-law. I wasn't sure the Fates would permit me two such experiences. I glanced down at the engagement ring he'd given me and smiled. We'd work it out.

"I heard from a friend at the National Weather Service that it looks like an EF-5 tornado touched down in River Bend," Frank said. "They aren't sure if we got hit by the tornado or just the winds here in North Harbor because there isn't as much damage around here, mostly downed trees and power lines. He said we were lucky. I wasn't worried until I saw the damage to the library."

"The North Harbor Library?" I asked.

"Didn't you see it?"

"No, there were so many power lines down we had to take a detour."

He shook his head. "It was the perfect sequence of events. The wind blew over an electric pole that fell on the water main. The building flooded and destroyed a ton of books."

The thought of all of those books getting damaged gripped my heart, and I gasped.

Frank squeezed my hand. "Thankfully, no one was injured, and the books can be replaced."

He was right. North Harbor Library was a small library and didn't have a rare books collection. Anything of significance had been moved to MISU's library years ago. Still, the library served a vital function in the community. It wasn't just a place for locals to read books. North Harbor Library provided ESL and literacy classes, assistance with résumés, guest speakers, and a host of other services.

"When I was young, my best friend and I used to walk to that library at least two times every week." I rested my head on Frank's chest.

Frank held me. "It'll be up and running in no time."

"Frank's right," Nana Jo said.

"It'll probably be better than ever," Jenna said. "That library was old and needed a lot of work. With any luck, they'll be able to use the insurance money to get the wiring, heating and air-conditioning, and computer systems updated."

I sniffed. "Well, I'm going to reach out to the librarian, Charlotte Simmons. Maybe there's something I can do to help."

"I'm sure they won't turn away help, but just be careful," Jenna said.

"Why? It's a library, not a prison. I'm sure it'll be fine. You're just still bitter because they asked you to do that one-hour legal clinic, and now eight months later, you're still volunteering."

"I don't mind volunteering, but I hate being voluntold." Jenna folded her arms across her chest. "And Charlotte Simmons called my boss and told them what a wonderful program I started, and now I'm stuck giving pro bono legal advice every week."

"You love doing pro bono work," Nana Jo said. "What's the problem?"

"The problem is, I like doing things on my own time and schedule. I agreed to a one-hour talk that has turned into four hours of free legal advice every week."

"Couldn't you just say no?" Frank asked.

"I've said *NO* multiple times, but Charlotte Simmons reminds me of the Mother Superior at St. Agnes's."

St. Agnes Catholic School for Girls was a small school within walking distance of our childhood home. We weren't Catholic, but my mom insisted that we attend. We got a good education and learned lessons that shaped our characters. Unlike many of our friends who had attended Catholic schools and shared horror stories of nuns who were martinets of discipline, the sisters of St. Agnes were the opposite. St. Agnes's nuns were sweet, kindhearted paragons of virtue. The principal, Sister Honorina, was barely five feet tall with soft brown eyes and a fondness for chocolate that bordered on obsession. She always believed the best of us, and whenever we did anything wrong, she took it personally. Most of us would rather leap off a cliff than admit to not living up to the standard that Sister Honorina held us to. The graduates of St. Agnes were well behaved, not because we were innately good, but because we didn't want to disappoint Sister Honorina.

"Maybe they're related," I said.

Jenna shook her head. "Nope. I asked."

Tony turned away to hide the smile that broke out on his face. I didn't even try to hide mine.

"Don't you dare laugh. You're my sister, so I'm going to give you a piece of advice. If you want to help the North Harbor Library, make an anonymous donation. Give cash. Donate furniture. Books. Whatever. But, if you value your mental peace and well-being, do NOT provide an open invitation, or you'll find yourself tied to that library for life and probably in the middle of some political intrigue."

I laughed. "Political intrigue? Are you joking? What kind of intrigue, political or otherwise, could there be involved with the North Harbor Library?"

A limb from the oak tree chose that exact moment to fall, and I wondered if it was an omen, but I shook it off.

Chapter 2

It's not often that I admit to my older sister that she was right. However, when I stopped by the North Harbor Library the next day, I met Charlotte Simmons. She was in her early fifties, with soft fluffy hair and soft gray eyes. When I introduced myself and explained that I wanted to help, her eyes filled with tears, and she gave me an adoring look as though I'd just offered her a kidney.

"Mrs. Washington, I'm just overwhelmed that a successful, busy businesswoman like yourself would go out of your way to help us. I'm at a loss for words." She pulled a lacy handkerchief from her sleeve and dabbed at her eyes.

"I'm happy to help." I slid a check across the counter. "Please let me know if there is anything else that I can—"

"I hate to ask because you've already been so generous, but . . . well, there is one thing that you could do." She tucked the check into a drawer and coughed.

"Sure. Whatever you need."

"It's just that we have several book clubs that meet at our library, and with the library closed . . . well, they don't have meeting space. Would it be asking too much to ask if they could meet at your bookstore?"

I released the breath I'd been holding. I wasn't sure what I thought she would ask, but this was a piece of cake. "Of course, sure. I'd be glad to host some of your book clubs. My bookstore isn't huge, and there are a few book clubs that already use my meeting room for their meetings, but I'm sure we can work out the details."

She beamed. "Oh, Mrs. Washington, you've just given me the best gift ever. I can't explain what a relief this is to know that our dedicated readers will have a place to continue meeting."

"I'm glad to help, and I will even give the book club members a discount if they want to buy books."

She gasped. "That's wonderful. You're a saint."

I felt the heat go up my neck. "Well, it's only temporary. After all, they'll be coming back here once the library re-opens."

I expected Mrs. Simmons to agree with me and provide the usual reassurances. *Of course, rest assured this is just a temporary arrangement. We wouldn't dream of imposing on your generosity for long,* etc., etc. So, it was a surprise when she merely smiled and then quickly turned away.

I walked outside into the sunshine with a strange flutter in the pit of my stomach, but I pushed the anxiety aside as I climbed into my Ford Escape and drove back to my bookstore.

Nana Jo had everything under control when I arrived, so I headed down the street to Frank's to grab lunch for both of us.

From the outside, North Harbor Café was deceptively small. However, when you entered, you saw that the building was deep and seemed to go on forever. Since the opening, it had been popular for good food and great service and always had a crowd. Today was no different.

I walked around the people waiting for tables. The hostess recognized me and glanced toward the bar.

Frank Patterson was behind the bar making drinks.

I walked over to the end of the bar and waited.

When Frank saw me, he smiled and pulled a large pitcher of water with lemons from the fridge. He poured the glass and set it in front of me before leaning across and giving me a kiss on the cheek. He lingered close long enough to whisper a few comments that made me giggle like a schoolgirl before leaning back. "Tell me the truth. You're here because you couldn't resist my charm, right?"

"If by charm you mean corn chowder and BLTs minus the T, then you are correct."

"I'll take what I can get." He laughed and headed toward the kitchen.

"Make it two," I said.

He nodded and hurried to the kitchen.

Frank could have entered my order into his computer system so that one of the chefs could have prepared it, but he always liked to make my orders himself. That simple act of care was just one of the many reasons I fell in love with him.

He was back in record time. I must have been smiling because he asked, "What? Is there mayo on my nose?"

I leaned across and kissed his nose. "I was just thinking how lucky I am."

He handed me my order. "If you're a good girl, you might just find a little something extra in your bag. Are you sure you don't want to come with me?"

Frank was leaving for a short trip to visit his mother, and he'd asked me to come along. It would be my first time meeting my soon-to-be mother-in-law. "As appealing as that sounds? I'm going to pass."

He grinned. "You're going to have to meet her sooner or later."

"I'll take later, thank you," I joked. "Seriously, I think you need to spend a little time with your mom. I'll meet her before the wedding. I promise." I gave him a kiss and whispered something that made a flush rise up his neck.

My flirting skills had improved dramatically since Frank and I first started dating. However, he had a restaurant full of people, and I needed to get back to work. So, we cut it short. I thanked him again for the food and hurried out.

Back at the bookstore, I took care of the customers so Nana Jo could eat and enjoy her lunch break. She rarely took a full hour, and when she was done, I ate. We worked the rest of the day in relative peace with a steady stream of customers. At the end of the day, we cleaned up and got the store ready for the next day.

"I'm going to curl up with a new thriller, *All Her Little Secrets* by Wanda M. Morris," Nana Jo said, holding up the book. "I started reading it, and can't put it down." She headed upstairs.

The best part about owning a mystery bookshop was access to so many great books. That was one of the main reasons my late husband, Leon, and I dreamed of owning one. The reality wasn't the romanticized dream where we sat around reading books and talking to mystery lovers all day. Owning a bookstore was hard work. Keeping track of inventory, stocking shelves, and dealing with customers, who weren't always kind, were just some of the issues. However, I still loved walking down the aisles and seeing shelves full of books. I loved the brightly colored covers and the smell of new books. Sitting in my bookstore, especially at night, always made me feel as though I was wrapped in a warm blanket.

I woke Snickers and Oreo and let them out to take care of business. Oreo was still a bit clingy, but he was almost back to his normal self. Snickers bounced back faster and was just as entitled as ever. Humans were here to serve, and I was her chief servant, here to do her bidding in exchange for unconditional love. That seemed fair to me.

I was just about to head upstairs when someone began pounding on the front door.

We were closed, and I didn't usually open up after hours. In fact, I was tempted to ignore the person. I'd locked the door myself and flipped the sign from OPEN to CLOSED. However, the pounding continued. I headed for the stairs but had a flashback to another time when someone pounded on my door and I'd denied him entry. He'd been found dead in my courtyard the very next morning. I wasn't a superstitious person, but I also didn't want to tempt fate twice. I turned the light back on and headed to the door. Based on the vigor, someone was obviously in distress.

I located my cell phone and tapped 9-1-1, careful not to push "send," and kept it in my hand as I walked toward the door.

Standing at the front door was Delia Marshall. Delia and I weren't acquainted, but I'd stared at her face every Sunday morning when I opened the Entertainment section of the local newspaper. Delia was one of North Harbor's most famous residents and a literary icon. She was a highly respected and syndicated book reviewer whose reviews were printed in the *Chicago Tribune*, *Washington Post*, and the *New York Times*. A review from Delia Marshall could make or break a debut author, like me.

I hurried to the door and fumbled to unlock it quickly. I swung the door open and smiled broadly. "I'm sorry, we're closed, but—"

Delia Marshall was short, stout, and reminded me of a linebacker on the MISU Tigers football team. She was solid as a rock and moved like a force of nature.

I hurriedly stepped aside to keep from getting run over. Snickers had to scramble to avoid getting crushed and yelped, similar to a driver tooting their car's horn to alert a motorist and prevent a collision.

Delia didn't stop until she was inside and leaning against the counter. Then, she turned and gave Snickers a *how dare you* scowl.

Snickers growled and curled her lip, exposing her teeth in a way that I had rarely seen my timid poodles do before. Oreo barked and lunged as though he was ready to take a piece of Delia's flesh.

I quickly scooped up both poodles and hurried out the back of the bookstore. I put them outside in the courtyard and closed the door. The volume of noise lessened dramatically, and the barking was a distant echo. I rushed back to the bookstore, prepared to apologize profusely for my poodles' behavior, but Delia was nowhere to be found.

I walked around and noticed a light on in the back room. When I got to the room, I found the door open and Delia Marshall seated at the head of the table.

"Mrs. Marshall, I don't think we've been formally introduced. My name is—"

She waved away my introductions. "I wouldn't be here if I didn't know who you were."

Stunned, I hesitated for a moment to regroup. I took a deep breath. "Of course, first, I'd like to apologize for my dogs. Normally, they're very well behaved and love people. I think they were surprised to see—"

"I don't like dogs. And dogs don't like me. You'll need to keep them locked up." She glanced around the room with her nose scrunched up as though she had just gotten a whiff of something one of the poodles had left behind. "Is this the biggest space you have?"

"Yes. I'm sorry, but the bookstore isn't huge." I wasn't sure why I was apologizing again, this time for the size of my building.

"I suppose it'll have to do." She hoisted herself up. "We'll take it."

"Excuse me?"

"Are you hard of hearing?"

"No, ma'am, but I don't understand . . . you'll take what?"

"The space. The Mystery Mavens Book Club meets on the first Sunday of the month at one thirty." She marched past me toward the door. "We're a small but prestigious group of committed mystery lovers. Writers. Academics. Book reviewers. Award-winning journalists. And, of course, me. I'm the leader of the group, and I'm proud to say that I've created a cultured, knowledgeable group with the ability to wield a great deal of power in the crime-writing community." She flicked an imaginary piece of dust from her shoulder. "You've heard of us, of course."

"Of course."

She nodded her approval and tilted her head. Her glasses slid down to the end of her nose and stopped. She glanced over the top of the rims and down her nose at me. "Then you'll know that we have *made* many crime writers. One good word from the Mystery Mavens, or yours truly, and your career will be set . . . or finished."

Her voice tone hadn't changed, but there was a threat that sent a shiver up my spine. Part of me wanted to throw her out of my bookstore. But I'd worked so hard on my book. I'd dreamed of being a published mystery writer for more years than I could remember. I'd written, edited, rewritten, and revised this book so many times I could recite it without looking at the pages. Even after it was sold, the book had been edited by my editor, then a copy editor, and finally a production editor. And I still woke up at night in a cold sweat, afraid we'd missed something. I had no idea publishing a book was so involved. Now, here stood Delia Marshall, essentially telling me she could crush my dreams before the book even made it to the stores.

"As much as I would love to believe that everyone will love my book, I know that's not true. However, I do hope that *readers* will judge it fairly." I smiled to soften the effect of the words, but based on the way my face felt, it might have been more of a grimace.

Delia sniffed. "You can't be that naïve."

I stared at her, unsure how to respond. I'd been so engrossed sparring with Delia Marshall that I hadn't heard Nana Jo join us.

"I wouldn't call it naïve to trust that if people read a book that they'll make a decision based on their own personal experience rather than allow themselves to be swayed by others," Nana Jo said.

Delia snorted. "Most people are idiots. I have an IQ of over two hundred, and it's my responsibility—nay, my burden to tell people what books are worthy of reading and which ones should be shunned."

I could tell by the flash in Nana Jo's eyes that this discussion was about to move from simmering to a rolling boil. Delia Marshall must have felt it, too, because she pulled her purse onto her shoulder, put her head down, and marched toward the door.

"I don't have time to educate you both. I've got things to do." She marched out into the bookstore and headed toward the front door. "We'll be by tomorrow. No need to go overboard to impress the group. A light lunch and cocktails will be fine with coffee and dessert." She yanked the door open and bounded out with the same energy as the tornado that had blown through just one day earlier.

"Whose house landed on her back?" Nana Jo asked.

"That was the famous book reviewer, Delia Marshall." I flopped down in a chair and buried my head in my arms. "Her columns get picked up by the Associated Press and appear in hundreds, maybe even thousands of newspapers all over the world. And she hates me, my dogs, and my book."

"She hasn't even read your book."

"It doesn't matter. I'm doomed."

"Don't be overly dramatic. She's just a pompous windbag who thinks more highly of herself than she ought to."

"Ugh," I groaned.

Nana Jo must have noticed how miserable I was and decided to take pity on me. She patted my back. "Don't worry, Sam. You've worked too hard to have your book torpedoed by the wicked witch of North Harbor. There's one way to tame a savage beast like that."

"How?" Without lifting my head, I turned to get a better look at my grandmother.

"Through her stomach. If she wants a 'light lunch,' well, we'll pull out all the stops. You'll get that talented fiancé of yours to whip up his famous orange cake and make some of that chicken salad with the grapes. That'll do the trick."

"You might just be onto something." I sat up. "I could make some scones, and I can take one of those jars of clotted cream I've been saving for my book signing."

"You'll have that bobcat purring like a kitten in no time." Nana Jo patted me on the back and headed upstairs.

Even though I wrote mysteries, my imagination wasn't big enough to imagine Delia Marshall purring, but Frank's orange cake was moist and delicious, and no one would be able to hold a grudge when faced with cake, scones, and clotted cream.

I let Snickers and Oreo back inside, and we followed my grandmother upstairs. My head was swimming, and I was wound up like a spring. It would be quite a while before I settled down enough to sleep. My only hope was to expel my nervous energy by spending some time in the British countryside.

⌒﹏﹏

Wickfield Lodge, English Country Home of
Lord William Marsh
1939

Lady Elizabeth Marsh sat on the overstuffed sofa of the large but cozy library in the home she shared with her husband, Lord William Marsh. The wood parquet floors were covered with large carpets that made for a comfortable foundation for her great-nephew, Lord William Carlston, as he lay on his back, attempting to shove his entire foot into his mouth.

Lady Elizabeth smiled as she glanced around at the faces of her family. Her husband, Lord William, the 8th Duke of Hunsford, sat in his favorite chair chomping on the stem of his pipe, while Cuddles, the duke's faithful but aging Cavalier King Charles spaniel, curled up at his feet.

Lord William and Lady Elizabeth hadn't been blessed with children of their own, but when Lord William's younger brother, Peregrin Marsh, and his wife, the beautiful Lady Henrietta Pringle, were both killed in a car accident, the duke and Lady Elizabeth had raised their two young daughters, Penelope and Daphne, as their own. Now, both girls were grown and married. Like old times, Lady Elizabeth watched her nieces and cousin sitting on the floor as she'd watched them for years. Only this time, their small family had more than doubled in both numbers and love.

Lady Penelope Carlston sat on the floor with her husband, Lord Victor Carlston. The raven-haired Lady

Penelope looked lovingly down on her small son. Her sister, Lady Daphne, leaned her blond head down and made an outlandish face, crossing her blue eyes, and puffed her cheeks out in an effort to garner a laugh from her nephew. Lady Daphne's husband, Lord James Fitzwilliam Browning, the 15th Duke of Kingsfordshire, stared lovingly down at his wife from his seat next to Lady Elizabeth. Lady Clara Trewellen-Harper, technically Lady Elizabeth's cousin but always more like a sister to Daphne and Penelope, sat cross-legged on the floor blowing kisses and talking gibberish to her young cousin, while her boyfriend, Detective Inspector Peter Covington, looked lovingly at his betrothed.

Lady Elizabeth gazed at her family and said a silent prayer of thanks. She was by the massive fireplace. Warm and snug, she glanced out a nearby window at the darkness as rain pounded against the windows and the winds howled and rattled the glass. She wondered how long they could keep the darkness from infiltrating her family circle. The storm raging outside seemed like a reflection of the dark forces that threatened to ravage the British homeland that she loved so much.

"Aunt Elizabeth, what do you think? I think Little William has his father's chin and my ears, don't you?"

Lady Elizabeth returned from her dark musings. "Well, dear, it's hard to tell with his foot in his mouth like that."

"That's exactly what makes him look so much like his father," Lord James said, smiling. "I've also seen him stick his foot in his mouth."

The door opened, and the Marsh family butler, Thompkins, wheeled in a cart laden with tea. He pushed the cart in front of Lady Elizabeth and bowed. He waited stiffly and silently to assist in distributing the tea.

Lady Elizabeth sat aside the fluffy blue yarn that she was knitting, poured tea, and handed it around.

"I've heard your cousin's trip was a great success," Lord James Browning said casually.

"Do you think he'll be able to come down for the christening?" Lady Penelope asked.

"Who can say?" Lady Elizabeth said, passing a cup of tea to her niece. "But given the state of affairs, I can't imagine it would be prudent or safe for the king to venture far from Windsor."

Lord William huffed on his pipe. "Bloody Nazis would like nothing better than to take out the king. Glad he's back on British soil. That's what. Touring the empire's all good and well in times of peace, but these are dark times."

"Oh, let's not talk about the Nazis or war or anything bad. I just can't stand it. The newspapers and the wireless are full of nothing but doom and gloom and predictions of war." Lady Clara wiped away a tear. "I just want to talk about chubby babies, tea, and parties."

The conversation returned to plans for young William's christening.

When the tea was distributed, Thompkins turned and left, silently closing the door behind him.

Lord Browning leaned close to Lady Elizabeth. "I know King George very much wants to attend the christening, but . . . it just isn't safe for him to travel."

"I do understand, but . . . well, it's in times like these that you want to be around your family more than ever. Who knows when . . ."

The duke reached over and clasped Lady Elizabeth's hand. "I understand. It's just a matter of time until we will all be called into action, and who knows when we will be able to enjoy quiet evenings with family again."

Thompkins opened the door and entered the library. "Telephone for your ladyship."

The Marshes' always prim and proper butler stood taller and more rigid than normal. Something in his eyes led Lady Elizabeth to ask, "Who could possibly be calling at this hour?"

"His Majesty, the King."

Chapter 3

For years, Sundays had been the time that I spent with my mom. Early morning church and then a trip to the movies, shopping, or whatever. Afterward, I would drop my mom at home and spend the next few hours reminding myself that I was an adult, not a child, and regaining my emotional equilibrium. Since my mom married Harold, our Sunday outings involved more people. Which actually worked out great and helped dilute my mom's super-invasive motherhood and its effect on me. Alone, my mother was too concentrated for my insecurities. Now that she and Harold were in Australia, Sundays were our day to connect as a family. Before leaving, Harold bought each member of the family an Echo Show. He didn't want our connection to be limited by the size of our cell phone screens or our cell phone packages. I wasn't the most technologically savvy member of my family and had resisted all of the devices that the younger generation used regularly. My technology-loving grandmother had other reasons for resisting.

"I don't like the idea of She-Who-Must-Not-Be-Named being all up in my business," Nana Jo whispered.

"Do you mean Alexa?"

"Shhh. Don't say her name." She glanced around suspiciously.

I whispered, "Why not, and why are we whispering?"

She glanced at the Echo Show. "Because *she* listens to our conversations."

"So? Who's she going to tell?"

"That's the most important question of all."

I smiled. "I never would have taken you for one of those conspiracy theorists who think the government is always listening."

"Oh, big deal. I could care less if the government listened to my conversations. Those bozos deserve to hear what I really think of the way they're managing our country."

"Then who?"

"It's them . . . those Larry Tate and Darrin Stephens people who listen to your conversations."

I frowned. "Larry Tate and Darrin Stevens . . . Aren't those the men from the *Bewitched* television show?"

She nodded. "Exactly. One minute you're having a conversation and just happen to mention that you need socks and toilet paper. The next thing you know, every ad that pops up on your computer has something to do with socks and toilet paper. I tell you, Sam, they're listening to us and using our words to market and sell."

I wanted to laugh, but I suspected she was right. I'd noticed something similar on my cell phone.

Now that my mom was gone, I thought I'd skip the early morning service and sleep late, but I found myself getting up and making my way to the church at eight o'clock even without my mom. Our church had grown substantially and underwent a few growing pains. The older members of the church preferred traditional hymns, while the younger congregants liked more upbeat music. The compromise was that the early service adhered to the traditional format with hymns and the later service was more upbeat. I enjoyed them both, but I found comfort in those time-honored hymns. Although I wasn't ready to admit it even to myself, I felt a connection to my mom whenever I attended the early service. It was almost as though she were there with me, reminding me to *sit up straight*, *mind your posture*, and *pay attention*. In my mid-thirties, I didn't think I needed or wanted that connection to my mom. I was wrong.

On a practical note, early service gave me a lot more time in the day to get everything done that I'd left undone. Besides, I had a feeling I was going to need all of the spiritual guidance and support I could get to manage Delia Marshall and the Mystery Mavens Book Club today.

I made stops at two grocery stores, a bakery, and the only florist that was open on Sundays in North Harbor before heading home. By the time I pulled into the garage, I was feeling peaceful and serene. Nana Jo was awake and sitting at the breakfast bar reading the Sunday newspaper and drinking coffee, but based on the grunt she gave when I walked into the kitchen, it was clear that the coffee had yet to soothe the savage beast.

Experience told me that keeping the conversation to a minimum would be best. So, I returned her grunt and got busy. Scones were surprisingly easy to make . . . well, easy once Dawson told me to freeze the butter and stop overworking the dough. While I wasn't in the same class as my assistant when it came to baked goods, I could hold my own where scones were concerned. I whipped up a batch and had them on the counter in my best tiered display platter in record time.

Nana Jo took a big whiff. "Those smell amazing. I don't suppose you could spare one for your favorite grandmother?"

"You're my only grandmother." I laughed as I put one of the scones and a dollop of strawberry preserves and double Devon cream onto a plate and slid it across the counter to her.

She slathered the scone with the cream and then the strawberry preserves and took a bite. She closed her eyes and moaned.

I released a sigh. My grandmother loved me, but she would have told me if my scones weren't up to par.

"Those are as good as the ones we had at Harrod's," she said around a mouthful of the pastry, and took a sip of coffee to wash it down.

"I doubt that, but thank you for saying it anyway. Now let's just hope that they're up to Delia Marshall's standards."

"Pshaw. I don't think Delia Marshall's turned away very many pastries, based on her size—"

"Nana Jo, that's not nice."

She waved away my comment. "Besides, I'd say beggars can't be choosy. Regardless, those scones are fit for royalty."

"When it comes to mystery reviewers, Delia Marshall is royalty."

Nana Jo picked up her paper. "I was just reading her review of that thriller I stayed up half the night finishing."

"Did she like it?"

"What's not to like? She gave it a positive review, which it deserves."

Something in her voice told me there was more. "What?"

"She gave the book a good review, but she also gave that newest tome by S. M. Themonéy a positive review."

"Themonéy has a lot of fans who love his books."

"Book, not books. That fossil's been writing the same book for the past ten years. He changes the names and the setting, but it's the same book with the same plot, and you know it."

"It's a formula that's worked for him."

"I read his last book, and at one point, he forgot the name of his protagonist and called him the same as the protagonist in his previous book."

I shivered. "I would have hoped his editor would have found that."

"Editor? What editor? He's just using search and replace to update the names and settings. Why would you need an editor for that?"

I used to be a huge fan of Themonéy, but Nana Jo was right. In the last few years, he'd barely changed more than the characters' names and locations but had doggedly stuck to the same storyline. In my younger days, I would have left a scathing review of the book, convinced that it was my duty to alert other unsuspecting readers. Now that I was about to publish my first book, I'd had a change of heart. Having labored over my book for years, I felt like a mother who's just spent forty-eight hours in labor only to have someone tell you that your baby is ugly. I'd gone back and removed all of the one-star reviews I'd ever given, choosing to adopt the motto, *If you can't say something nice, don't say anything at all*, as my standard. Was it the right thing to do? Who knows? Everyone is entitled to their opinion, and we have the right to voice that opinion. Lately, I couldn't help wondering about the effect some of those blatantly honest reviews had on the authors who had toiled to produce a work of fiction only to be told their book's best use was as a liner for a birdcage. My agent had attempted to help prepare me for negative reviews by showing me some of the negative reviews that had been written about Shakespeare, Hemingway, and even the Bible. I know everyone doesn't like the same things, and there would be a number of people who wouldn't like my book, *Murder at Wickfield Lodge*, but it was my baby, and I loved it. Hearing others hated it would hurt. So, I refused to badmouth S. M. Themonéy . . . at least not in writing.

"Maybe Delia really liked that plotline?" I said weakly.

"Humph. She must. Plus, she trashed the mystery by Martha Chiswick and Evelyn Randolph, and they're not only local but are members of the Mystery Mavens." Nana Jo held up the book that was beside her plate.

"Is it good? I haven't had a chance to read it yet. It's on the top of my to-be-read pile. I like supporting local artists, so I ordered a case. I figured maybe they'd sign copies." I shrugged. "Who knows, maybe they'll want to hold a book reading or something."

"That was nice." Nana Jo finished off her scone and turned back to the newspaper.

"I know it wouldn't be right to give a positive review just because you're friends or because you know someone, but this review was vicious." Nana Jo held out the newspaper for me to read.

I read the review and winced. "Ouch. That wasn't just a review. It was a crucifixion." I sat down on the barstool. "I'm doomed. If she said that about people she knows and likes, I can only imagine what she'll say about my book."

"Stop worrying. Delia Marshall is only great in her own mind. Readers are smarter than she gives them credit for. You know as much, if not more, about mysteries than that pretentious twit. You know your audience. You run a mystery bookshop, for Christ's sake. Besides, you've successfully solved several mysteries. I doubt that Miss-I-Have-An-IQ-Over-Two-Hundred Delia Marshall ever solved a murder."

"Thank you, Nana Jo. I appreciate the pep talk, but . . ."

She put her hand on her hip. "But what?"

"You're my grandmother, and you're just the slightest bit biased." I kissed her cheek.

"Wrong."

"What? I thought you liked my book?"

"I'm your grandmother, and I'm completely biased in your favor. But I've been reading mysteries for sixty years, and I know good writing when I see it. Your book is good. I wouldn't let you put yourself out there if I didn't think it was better than that claptrap that S. M. Themonéy regurgitates year after year."

My family, especially my sister, were more of the tough love variety, so I knew that she would indeed have told me, albeit kindly, if my book wasn't ready, so I tucked that knowledge in my back pocket and worked on my scone and charcuterie presentation.

I took my best china and glassware downstairs and decorated my conference room in preparation for the Mystery Mavens. I brought books to use as platters for the food and additional decorations. Just as I finished, Frank arrived with his offerings. When he had heard about my altercation with Delia, he promised to help. He came with chicken salad, homemade bread, a citrus salad, and orange cake with warm caramel sauce. The buffet overflowed with delicious food, and with the freshly baked bread and cake, it smelled as good as it looked.

"Have I told you lately how much I love you?"

Frank smiled. "It's been a few hours, but I could stand to hear it again."

I took a few minutes to show him my appreciation. When he came up for air, he fanned himself. "Are you sure you don't need some more food? If you give me a couple of hours, I can have a prime rib that will melt in your mouth."

I laughed. "Don't be silly. You are amazing, and I love you, not just because you're an excellent cook, but because you are always so thoughtful and generous and—"

He kissed me. "You're going to give me a big head."

"But it's true."

"Food is what I do. I love to cook and to feed people, especially the people I love. This is easy."

"Well, I want you to know how much I appreciate you."

I heard the bell announcing that someone was entering the bookstore just as Frank's cell phone rang and he had to leave to take care of a problem at the restaurant.

When I came out to greet my customers, I was shocked to see an animated conversation between Delia Marshall and two other women.

"That's enough, Martha. You're lucky that I bothered to review your book at all. My shelves are overflowing, and I pushed aside other books to read your . . . little book."

Martha Chiswick's cheeks flushed, and her eyes flashed. "If you were going to trash the book, why bother at all?"

Delia gave a snide smile. "They do say that *any publicity is better than no publicity.* Millions of people read my column. A mention from me, good or bad, will draw some attention your way. Some folks are bound to pick up a copy just to see what all the fuss is about."

"Fuss? You called our book trite and said you'd have to be dumb as a box of rocks not to see who the killer was. Isn't that right, Evelyn?" Martha turned to the other woman, who looked as though she was ready to burst into tears.

"*Dios mío,*" Evelyn said quietly. "You all but named the killer in your review. People won't bother reading a mystery when they already know whodunit."

"Well, you can't blame me for stating the obvious," Delia said. "I'm a journalist with an obligation to my readers." She shrugged. "You two made your bed. Now lie in it."

A man with a felt fedora pulled down rakishly over his eyes entered. He quickly assessed the situation and smiled. "Ah, looks like the tide has turned, and the authors have come for their revenge." He gave a wicked grin in Delia's direction. "You'd better watch your back, Delia love. I personally never believed that drivel that says the pen is mightier than the sword. There's nothing like a sharp sword to cut a critique down to size. And if you don't watch your back, you're likely to find the truth of the matter."

Chapter 4

I stood there gaping. Did he really just say what I thought he did? Did he just threaten Delia? Surely, I didn't hear what I thought I did.

"Denver, you wouldn't have the guts to wield that sword, so you'd best just stick to the pen," Delia said.

After an uncomfortable silence, Denver laughed. "Right again, Delia my love."

Again, I was so engrossed I didn't notice Nana Jo. I jumped when she said, "That's Denver Benedict."

"*The* Denver Benedict?" I said. "Pulitzer Prize–winning Denver Benedict?"

She nodded. "I wonder how he got roped into this tragedy."

Delia spotted me, and I didn't have long to ponder.

"Samantha, come meet our illustrious book club members."

I tried to move, but my legs were frozen in place. Nana Jo gave me a gentle push and propelled me over to the group.

Delia said, "This is Samantha Washington, proprietor of Market Street Mysteries Bookshop, and our host."

I smiled and willed myself to say something, but no words came.

If Delia noticed, she didn't let on. Instead, she turned to Denver. "This degenerate is the world-renowned, award-winning journalist and author Denver Benedict."

I extended my hand.

Denver Benedict bowed and kissed my hand.

If anyone else had done that, I would have been annoyed. However, I found myself giggling . . . actually giggling. I knew I was behaving like a teenager with a crush, but to be honest, I have crushed on Denver Benedict's intelligent, snarky, tragically romantic heroes for decades.

Nana Jo put an arm around my shoulders, perhaps to prevent me from attempting to execute a full-blown curtsy. She extended her other hand. "I'm Sam's grandmother, Josephine Thomas, but everyone calls me Nana Jo."

He puckered up to kiss Nana Jo's hand, but she pulled her hand away from his lips and gave his hand a few pumps. "I'm encouraged to see men in the Mystery Mavens—"

Benedict opened his mouth to respond, but Delia intervened. "The uneducated believe 'mavens' is a feminine word, but it means—"

"Uneducated? Why you—"

Nana Jo lunged, but Stevie Wonder could have seen that coming, and I stepped between Nana Jo and Delia Marshall. "How incredibly interesting, but we—"

"A connoisseur, adept, virtuoso, and genius are just a few synonyms that accurately touch upon what we do."

"I know what it means," Nana Jo growled, but that didn't stop Delia.

"Similar to the Bilderberg Group, the Mystery Mavens are more than a mere group of people who read and discuss books. Oh no. We're leaders in the genre . . . influencers." Delia stopped to take a breath.

I saw my opening and moved in. "How intriguing. I don't think I've met these other women." I flashed Delia a big smile and turned toward the two women, careful to maintain my position blocking Delia from my grandmother. Although, considering that Nana Jo was a martial arts expert, I knew that she could have flipped me and taken out Delia Marshall if she wanted, but I was counting on the fact that my grandmother wouldn't want to hurt me just to flip Delia Marshall flat on her back.

Delia looked irritated that I'd interrupted her monologue. She had no idea how close she'd just come to death, but she turned and continued the introductions. "These women are Martha Chiswick and Evelyn Randolph. They've both just released their debut mystery. Perhaps you saw my review in the newspaper?"

I smiled and extended my hand. "Ladies, I'm pleased to meet you both. Local authors are always popular, and I'm sure my patrons will be excited to read your new book. So, I bought a case. Could I prevail on you to sign them?"

The shock on Martha's and Evelyn's faces contrasted with the sour expression on Delia's.

"Oh, that's so kind. We'd love to sign them." Martha turned to her friend, who nodded vigorously.

"Great. Maybe if you have time after your meeting, you can do it then. Do you have a reading planned? If not, I'd love to host you."

I didn't think their smiles could have gotten bigger, but I was wrong. They beamed. Martha Chiswick was tall and thin with angular features. She looked to be in her mid-fifties with salt-and-pepper shoulder-length hair. She looked like a hippie with a long skirt that went to her ankles and sandals. Evelyn Randolph would only hit five feet tall if she stood on a box. She had a round face and a round belly. She had mousy brown hair and eyes and round rosy cheeks.

"Oh, a book reading," Evelyn said. "That would be lovely."

Delia looked as though she'd just sucked on a lemon. "Yes, well, there's no accounting for taste."

I chose to ignore Delia Marshall. "I think the local artist market is expanding. I just read in a publishing announcement that another local author just sold a big deal. Maybe we can have a panel featuring local mystery authors after his book releases. Do you know him? His name's Kincaid."

Delia Marshall snapped to attention. "Kincaid? Preston Kincaid?"

"Yes. I think that's it. He got a seven-figure deal and is negotiating the film rights. So, he may not want to do anything here, but I know people at MISU, and we might be able to do something there."

Delia's mind drifted away, but she was brought back to earth when someone came to the store. The door opened, and a tall, dark, handsome man with shoulder-length dreadlocks pulled back into a ponytail, gray eyes, and a British accent rushed into the bookshop. Dressed in denim jeans, with a stark white oxford shirt, and carrying a leather book bag, the newcomer glanced around and released a breath. "Brilliant. I was afraid I'd be late."

Delia's frown deepened. "You are late." She turned to me. "This is Dr. Geoffrey Allen, professor of criminal psychology. Dr. Allen isn't a member of Mystery Mavens. He's merely a guest . . . someone recommended to us. He's visiting with us on a trial basis." She turned to Dr. Allen. "Samantha Washington."

The twinkle in his eyes told me he not only recognized the insult, but he was also completely unfazed by it. He extended his hand. "Mrs. Washington, I have heard so much about you and have been looking forward to meeting you since I got here." My puzzled look spurred him to continue. "I believe you know my godmother, Ruby Mae Stevenson."

Ruby Mae Stevenson was one of my grandmother's closest friends. We shook hands. "Of course I know Ruby Mae. I'm so pleased to *finally* get a chance to meet you, Dr. Allen." I introduced Nana Jo.

He asked us to call him Geoff, which distracted Nana Jo from the daggers she was shooting in Delia's direction.

"Ruby Mae talks about you all the time," Nana Jo said. "She was so disappointed that you were out of the country during our trip to England. She wanted you to meet everyone, but congratulations. It's not every author who gets an opportunity to interview the pope."

"I tried to get the interview rescheduled, but His Holiness had a really tight schedule. It was that one shot or nothing."

"Of course you had to go. Ruby Mae understood, and she was so proud of you, and so are we."

Delia's neck snapped up to attention at the mention of the pope. "You interviewed *the* pope?"

Geoff shrugged. "His Holiness, Pope Francis, took an interest in my research and graciously agreed to a rare interview."

"Was that the interview that earned you a BAFTA?" Nana Jo asked.

Geoff held up his hands. "I was just one part of the team that earned that BAFTA. There were a host of men and women who'd worked for years on that project, and I was just fortunate enough to be in the right place at the right time."

"Pish posh. Don't be so modest." Nana Jo flashed a huge smile Delia's way. "The awards and accolades this young man has won are truly impressive." Nana Jo didn't say that Geoff was too good for the Mystery Mavens . . . at least not with words, but her meaning was clear.

Delia looked as though she'd swallowed glass but quickly shook it off. "Interesting, well, I did mention that Dr. Allen was *recommended* to us. But there will be plenty of time to discuss the logistics later. Right now we have business to discuss." She flung one side of her cape over her shoulder and marched like Napoleon toward the conference room.

I gave a quick overview of the food in the room and encouraged everyone to dig in.

I hung around for a few moments to ensure everyone had what they needed. I was pleased to see that the group enjoyed the food. With full mouths, the club members moaned and grunted approval of the fare. All except Delia, who cleaned her plate but remained silent.

Once I knew they were set, I left the group in peace to discuss . . . influence . . . or whatever they did in peace. Nana Jo looked relieved. She couldn't wait to get away from Delia. I couldn't help but feel a tad bit hurt not to be included. I wasn't a member of the Mystery Mavens, but I read mysteries. I read a *lot* of mysteries. I own a mystery bookshop. I'm also a soon-to-be-published mystery writer, which is more than I can say for Delia Marshall, and they were meeting at my bookshop. I mean, they could have offered me the opportunity to join their discussion since I was allowing them to meet at my shop for free while the library underwent repairs.

Nana Jo greeted a customer and then came over to where I was unpacking books and placing them on a shelf. "What's wrong?"

"Nothing."

I should have known better than to try to hide my feelings. My grandmother always could read me like a Mickey Spillane, Mike Hammer novel.

"Don't tell me you want to be involved in that tyrannical lunatic's book club because I don't believe it."

I stopped shelving books. "I don't want to be a part of the book club, but . . . it would have been nice to have been asked."

"You're better off not going. That woman would have

just made you mad, and you would have probably ended up clobbering her." Nana Jo picked up a hefty hardback book that was delivered. "This book is an anvil." She turned it over and looked at the title. "*The Complete Works of Agatha Christie.* Dear God. This is massive."

I smacked my head. "I remember now why Delia Marshall seemed familiar. She ordered the book. She called and custom-ordered it. I had it shipped from England."

"The shipping alone had to cost a small fortune."

"It was incredible. The book had to go through customs, and it's taken two months to get here. That's why I didn't re-member." I lifted the tome and nearly dropped it. "When it says complete works, they mean *everything.* This one book has all her sixty-six mysteries, three poems, fourteen short stories, sixteen plays, and two autobiographies. It even has the stories she wrote under her pen name, Mary Westmacott."

"All that and bound in leather. It had to cost a fortune. How much?"

"Twelve hundred dollars."

Nana Jo whistled.

"That's the leather-bound book, gold leaf pages, and she had her name engraved." I slid the book around to show. "Plus, there was packing, shipping, customs, and insurance."

"I'm sure it's worth every dollar. It's just a lot of dollars."

"She was *very* particular about the book. It had to be the *exact* edition and the *exact* publisher." I sat the book on the counter so I wouldn't forget to let Delia know it had arrived, and I could get paid for it. Twelve hundred dollars was a lot of money, not to mention the money I'd spent on food for the club meeting. Frank wouldn't charge me, but I was deter-mined to pay him out of the book proceeds.

The store wasn't crowded, but we had a steady stream of customers that kept us busy. Two hours later, I heard raised voices and stopped to figure out where they were coming from. It didn't take me long to figure it out. I apologized to my customer. Fred Yoder was a mystery lover and a regular. He usually stopped by about once or twice every month, always on Sundays with his West Highland terrier in a pooch pouch strapped to his chest.

I hurried to the conference room, twisted the knob, and entered without knocking. I stood for a brief moment to take in the scene. Delia Marshall was seated at the head of the table. A red-faced Evelyn Randolph stood over Delia. Her face was distorted by anger and her eyes bulged. She looked as though she would explode.

Martha Chiswick clutched her friend's arm. Geoff Allen appeared to be frozen in shock. Wide-eyed, he stared at the woman as though he couldn't believe what he was seeing. In a corner, Denver Benedict sat alone and laughed hysterically.

"What's going on in here?" I asked.

My presence diffused what appeared to be a volatile situation. Evelyn allowed herself to be led back to her seat by her friend. Denver Benedict abruptly stopped laughing and sat staring as though in a daze. Geoff Allen picked up the pitcher of lemon water I'd left and poured a glass. His hand shook, and some of the water spilled on the table.

"Well?" I glanced around the table and finally rested my gaze on Geoff Allen.

He took a drink of water and put his glass down. He took a deep breath. "It was—"

Delia stood. "The Mystery Mavens Book Club is a *private* meeting. Like Vegas, *What happens here, stays here*. This doesn't concern you."

"Are you kidding? I could care less about your *private meeting*, but this is my bookstore, my business, and my home. And anything that happens here concerns me."

Delia tossed her cape over her shoulder. "I received an advanced reader copy of your book. I haven't read it yet. I was afraid it might be a bit overly dramatic." She looked over the top of her glasses and down her nose at me. "Seems I might be right."

I can't imagine anything else that could have shocked me silent faster. I stared with my mouth open.

My hesitation gave Delia the edge she needed. "If you're worried about our group disrupting your customers, perhaps we should move upstairs for our next meeting. I understand you have a . . . decent space that should be more comfortable and private. It should also make it easier for you to provide *hot* food." She gave the folding chair a scowl and then marched out.

I stared at the door.

"I'm surprised no one has murdered that woman," I said. "She's absolutely despicable." I was so angry I was shaking.

Denver Benedict rose and walked toward the door. Before leaving, he turned and pointed a gnarled finger at me. "Young fool . . . only now, in the end, do you understand."

I was too shocked to catch the *Star Wars, Return of the Jedi* reference. I stared at the door. "You were right. She's lucky no one has killed her. I'm so furious, I could happily club her to death." I turned to Geoff Allen. "Are you going to tell me what happened?"

Before he could answer, there was a loud crash in the bookstore, which was followed by barking and growling, and not all of the growling was coming from my dogs.

I hurried out to the main bookshop and found Delia sitting on the floor, with Oreo cowering in a corner while Snickers barked and lunged. "Snickers, stop that." I bent down and scooped up both poodles.

"That's the last straw," Delia said. "Those mongrels attacked me. I am going to sue you for every dime you have." She struggled to get up.

I rushed the poodles to the door that led upstairs to my

apartment and made sure it was closed tightly behind me. When I returned, Delia was on her feet, but she was still screaming. "Mrs. Marshall, are you okay?"

She scowled. "Okay? Of course I'm not okay. And you're going to pay for—"

"Perhaps you should sit down and let me call an ambulance." I whipped out my cell phone.

"I don't need an ambulance. I need an attorney who will take you for all—"

"Please, Mrs. Marshall. We can discuss that later. My primary concern is your health. Now, where does it hurt?" I tapped 9-1-1.

"Were you listening? I told you I don't want an ambulance."

"Nine-one-one," the operator said. "What's your emergency?"

"Well, I have a customer who fell in my store, but she is refusing an ambulance," I said.

"That's right, I'm not paying for an ambulance to come and tell me what I already know!" Delia shouted. "I'm going to get an attorney who'll mop the floor with you."

I turned away. "Did you hear her? I'm not sure what to do."

"Is she bleeding?" the operator asked. "Can you see any signs of injury?"

I stared at Delia. "There's no blood, and I don't see any visible injuries, but she was on the ground, so I guess she could have broken something or have internal injuries."

"You really need to convince her to seek medical attention. At least have the EMTs check her to rule out anything internal."

"Mrs. Marshall, I really think—"

"That's your problem. You don't think. I've already told you that I have no intention of paying for an ambulance."

"If it's the money, I'll be glad to pay for the ambulance to make sure you're okay," I pleaded.

"Oh, you're darned right you're going to pay. When my attorney gets through with you, you'll pay big time. And he'll start by getting rid of those two rodents you call dogs."

"What? Are you implying that my dog bit you?"

"You saw them lunging at me. That dog probably has rabies. Only one way to find out. They'll take it and put it down and run tests."

My eyes started to blur, and I felt as though I was going to pass out. I might have if Nana Jo hadn't come up to support me.

"Sam, are you okay?" Nana Jo asked.

Delia saw the effect her words had, and she pounced on her advantage. "Dogs shouldn't be allowed in a retail establishment, and those two are dangerous. I'll personally see to it that—"

"You'll do no such thing. Now, sit down and shut up," Nana Jo said in the voice she'd used while teaching second grade. It was firm and brooked no opposition. The fact that she was close to six feet tall and over two hundred pounds didn't hurt either.

Delia sat, stunned.

I remembered the 9-1-1 operator. "Hello, are you still there?"

"Yes, ma'am, I'm still here." She paused for a moment. "May I ask, is that Delia Marshall?"

"Yes, it is. Do you know her?"

"Oh yes. We are very familiar with Mrs. Delia Marshall. I'm canceling the ambulance and sending the police. Mrs. Marshall prefers to use her own doctor for these incidents."

"Incidents?"

"A piece of advice. Get names, telephone numbers, and signed statements from any witnesses who saw the incident.

And hire a good attorney. I'd also recommend you get any surveillance footage you can. You'll thank me later."

"You sound like you've dealt with something like this before," I said cautiously.

"Let's just say this isn't my first rodeo. Good luck, ma'am."

I hung up. "She canceled the ambulance, but the police should be here shortly to take statements."

Delia hopped up. "The police . . . I don't have time to wait around for the police." She turned to Evelyn Randolph. "I'm going to need you to drive me home. I need to get some ice on my back."

Evelyn Randolph and Martha Chiswick helped Delia Marshall out of the shop and into a blue sedan. Once Delia was strapped in, they left just as the North Harbor patrol car pulled up.

"For someone who's injured, she sure managed to skedaddle out of here pretty quickly when you mentioned the police," Nana Jo said.

Martha Chiswick, Evelyn Randolph, Geoff Allen, and Denver Benedict were all in the conference room with me when Delia had her accident. Nana Jo and Fred Yoder were the only ones in the bookstore. Nana Jo wasn't paying attention, but Fred Yoder swore that Oreo and Snickers were scouring the floor for crumbs in the café area at the back of the bookstore. He claimed that when Oreo came near Delia, she kicked him, and he went flying into one of the bookshelves. When Snickers saw her brother under attack, she growled and lunged at Delia, but she never actually made contact. In backing away from Snickers, Delia tripped over the box of books I'd left on the floor and fell.

"Sam, this is all my fault," Nana Jo said. "I must have left the door open when I went upstairs to get my glasses."

I was furious that Delia had kicked Oreo. He was the sweetest, most loving creature on earth. He was curious and believed that all humans were his friend. Delia definitely was not. I was also secretly pleased that Snickers had acted out of concern for her brother. Most days, she barely tolerated him.

"This isn't your fault. It's my fault. I should never have agreed to allow the Mystery Mavens to meet here, especially after I saw how malicious Delia Marshall was. I was just afraid that she'd sink my book."

Nana Jo hugged me.

"Plus, as a pet owner, I'm responsible for my dogs," I said.

"Well, there's no way I'm going to stand by and let that woman hurt you, Snickers, or Oreo."

"I'm glad I got top billing in that list." I smiled and then pulled out my cell phone. "I guess it's time to swallow my pride and get this resolved."

"I sure hope you're not calling that woman to offer her some kind of settlement," Nana Jo said.

"Actually, I'm following the nine-one-one operator's advice. I'm calling my attorney." I punched the numbers on the phone. "Hello, Jenna. I need an attorney."

Chapter 5

Asking my sister for help was hard. It's not that I didn't think she could do it. She was an excellent attorney with a reputation of being a pit bull. And I didn't have a problem soliciting my sister's help for others. My problem was asking for my sister's help for myself. It isn't even that I didn't think she'd do it. I knew she would. My issues were related to thirty-plus years of little sister torture. Jenna was almost four years older than me, and despite the fact that I am an adult, it's only recently that I've realized I don't have to do everything she tells me. I've even said, *"You're not the boss of me."* Okay, maybe I haven't said it out loud and to her face (Nana Jo said saying it to Snickers and Oreo doesn't count), but I've certainly thought it. But in my little sister brain, asking my sister for help was like opening the door to big sister domination.

To Jenna's credit, she listened. That's another of my *little sister* issues. I felt that Jenna listened, really listened, to everyone except me. However, today was different, which made me nervous. "Okay, why are you so quiet? What's wrong?"

"I wish you had insisted on the ambulance. At least we could have had their assessment of her injuries."

"I tried, but—"

"Also, are you sure that Snickers didn't nip her?"

"That's what Mr. Yoder said. I didn't see it."

Silence.

"Jenna, you're scaring me. You don't honestly believe that Snickers bit her."

Silence.

"Jenna!"

"I'm not saying she did. But if Snickers scared her and she tripped over the box, then she could still blame her for any injuries . . . and . . ."

"And what?"

"Sam, she could sue. Michigan has very strict liability for dog bites. All responsibility is on the owner."

"But she's a ten-pound toy poodle. She's never bitten anyone, and she didn't bite Delia Marshall."

"Sam, I know. You're not going to want to hear this, but the law states that you could be charged with negligence. If Delia Marshall has injuries as a result of your dog, then you may be required to compensate her for all damages. Let me pull up the law."

I heard the faint sound of her keyboard. After a few moments, she began to read.

"To prove damages, Michigan law requires the injured party to prove that the dog caused injuries, the injured party was in a place they were lawfully allowed to be, including the dog owner's home as long as they have permission to be there. And they didn't provoke the dog to cause the attack."

I was stunned. "But Snickers didn't bite her."

"She doesn't have to bite to cause injuries. Delia Marshall could charge you with negligence, and it's possible that if a dog knocks someone down, you could be held liable. And, while I hate to mention it," Jenna said softly, "she could even bring criminal charges."

I wasn't sure when the tears started, but I couldn't stop them once they did. "But it's not fair. If Delia hadn't kicked Oreo, then Snickers never would have growled at her."

"Sam, I know this hurts, but it's better to know what we're up against. So, I'm going to give it to you straight." She paused. "I doubt that you will have to face criminal charges, but you could be faced with civil charges. It could be a long affair, and if this goes to a trial, you never know how a jury will respond. If you lose, it could be costly. It might be better to look for a solution that doesn't involve going to court."

"What are you suggesting? You think I should pay her?"

Silence.

"You do. You think I should pay her . . . settle out of court."

"I'm not telling you what to do. I need to do some more research. But the law is clear. You're liable for your dogs. Let me look into some of the recent cases. In the meantime, if Delia or her attorney calls, let me know. Do not answer any questions or give any statements unless I'm there." Jenna sighed. "Sam, I'm sorry. I know how much those dogs mean to you, but this is serious. I'll do everything I can, but there might not be anything I can do."

I hung up the phone with my sister and collapsed in a pool of tears.

When I finally stopped crying, I had a headache and was in no shape to work. Nana Jo sent me upstairs to rest.

The climb upstairs opened the waterworks again. By the time I made it to the top, I was midway to another meltdown. One look at Snickers and Oreo, who were waiting for me at the top of the stairs, took me the rest of the way to a full-blown meltdown. I picked up the poodles and squeezed them to my chest. Oreo wasn't a hugger and wiggled until he found a gap large enough for him to squeeze out of my arms. Snickers was always good for hugs when I needed comfort. She endured a good twenty minutes of my crying and sniveling. When I was completely out of tears, she licked my face with a ferocious vengeance. She was a persistent licker, and eventually, she had me laughing as I tried to fend her off. Laughing was a big mistake. I opened my mouth, and immediately she managed to lick me.

"Yuck. Snickers, that's icky."

She didn't stop until I managed to wiggle away.

Nana Jo hurried upstairs. "What's going on?"

"Nothing. Why do you ask?"

"One minute, you're crying your eyes out. The next, you're laughing hysterically." She stared. "I thought you were having an emotional breakdown."

"Sorry."

She didn't look like she believed me, but she eventually went back downstairs.

It took nearly an hour before I was calm enough to mention Delia's name without punching a pillow and mumbling a few words I'd learned from hanging out with my grandmother's friend Irma.

I had a major headache and went to my bedroom to take a nap.

I tossed and turned for about thirty minutes before I gave up on sleep and headed for my laptop.

⁓

Lady Elizabeth Marsh and Thompkins entered the long servants' dining room of Wickfield Lodge. A large rectangular oak table with matching chairs was in the center of the room and in front of a massive fireplace. At the other end of the room was a massive

AGA stove, prep table, and the new icebox. The Marsh family's cook, Mrs. Anderson, hadn't been a fan of the newfangled appliance when it first arrived, but she'd quickly been won over by the convenience.

The two footmen, Jim and Frank, and the maids, Flossie, Gladys, and Millie, stood quietly around the table. The girls glanced frequently from Lady Elizabeth to the housekeeper, Mrs. McDuffie, for direction. Mrs. Anderson and her daughter Agnes brought tea and the last of the servants' goodies to the table.

"Please sit down and enjoy your tea," Lady Elizabeth said. She smiled at the servants and waited while they complied with her request.

Everyone except Thompkins and Mrs. McDuffie sat and poured their tea. Lady Elizabeth knew that her presence would inhibit the staff, but she also didn't want their tea to get cold, so she hurried to share her news.

"I know that you've all been working hard to prepare for the christening of Lord and Lady Carlston's son, but there's been a bit of a change of plans."

Millie, the newest of the maids to join the group, bounced in her chair. "Oh, m'lady, if you tell me that His Majesty the King is actually going to be staying here, I think I'll faint."

Mrs. McDuffie frowned. "You will *not* faint, no matter what 'er ladyship 'as to tell you," she said sternly, and turned her attention to each of the young maids.

Millie colored and dropped her gaze. "Yes, ma'am."

Lady Elizabeth knew that the housekeeper ran a tight ship. Mrs. McDuffie was a stout, middle-aged woman with a freckled complexion and fluffy red hair that was thin and curly. She was stern but fair, but anything as unseemly as fainting would not be tolerated.

"Unfortunately, His Royal Highness is unable to travel at this time." She paused and watched as the disappointment registered. She knew that the staff had been working extremely hard to prepare for the possibility of a royal visit. Even though Lady Elizabeth was a cousin, the Marshes had never hosted a royal visit.

Gladys forced a smile to hide her disappointment. "They must be exhausted after traveling all the way to Canada and the United States."

"True, but His Majesty's reasons revolved more around safety. He wanted to come, but given the current state of affairs, it wasn't deemed safe."

Joseph Mueller entered the dining room by the back door but stopped when he saw the group was meeting and turned to leave.

"Joseph . . . Mr. Mueller, please stay," Lady Elizabeth said, smiling. "This concerns you, too."

Joseph Mueller quickly sat and glanced at Thompkins, his father-in-law, who merely stood straighter and taller.

"I was sharing that His Majesty will not be coming to Wickfield Lodge for the christening. Aware of the disappointment this will cause, His Majesty has suggested an alternative." She paused. "His Majesty has offered to host the christening at Windsor Castle."

The group was quiet for a few moments, and then there were general murmurs of good wishes and safe travels for the family.

"Well, that'll be a waste," the cook mumbled. "I've been preparing and baking for two weeks."

"I'm afraid I'm not explaining myself well." Lady Elizabeth smiled. "His Majesty, King George, has invited *all of us* to Windsor Castle for the christening." She turned to the cook. "We'll be taking everything you've prepared to the castle to serve the guests."

"Oh, m'lady, are you saying we're all going to Windsor Castle?" Gladys asked breathlessly.

Lady Elizabeth nodded. "The royal family wants to set a good example for the country and don't have quite the same number of staff at the moment. Plus, we know you've all worked so hard to prepare for a royal visit that we agreed it would be better if we brought our own staff, especially given the last-minute changes."

The room buzzed with excitement.

"You're taking all of us to Windsor?" Jim asked.

Lady Elizabeth smiled big and nodded. The servants erupted in whoops of joy and laughter as they joked about practicing their curtsies and bows.

The only person not excited was Joseph Mueller. Lady Elizabeth intercepted a puzzled look that Mueller shot toward his father-in-law.

The Marshes had engaged Mueller to teach Johan, Josiah, and Rivka, children from the Kindertransport the family was sheltering. The children didn't speak much English, and the Marshes' German was severely lacking. Thompkins's daughter, Mary, had married a Jewish scientist and teacher. They had graciously agreed to help with the language and everything necessary to help the family and staff adapt to the children's culture.

Lady Elizabeth knew that Mueller's political views were more liberal than their own. She wondered if he would oppose an opportunity to meet the king. "The children have been looking forward to the christening, so we were hoping you and Mary would come."

The young teacher's cheeks flushed. "We would be honored."

Mrs. McDuffie's normally ruddy complexion was even ruddier with excitement. "Lord, I never thought I'd get to meet the king, let alone go inside Windsor Castle." She frowned at the maids. "You girls better mind your p's and q's or so 'elp me, I'll . . ." She glanced at Lady Elizabeth and then scowled at the eager young maids.

Thompkins coughed.

Lady Elizabeth recognized that short, discreet cough as the butler's way to draw attention to his entrée into the conversation.

"Yes, Thompkins." Lady Elizabeth turned to the butler.

"M'lady, please forgive my impertinence, but if you're worried about the staff's behavior, I can assure you—"

Lady Elizabeth waved away his concerns. "Of course I'm not concerned. I have faith in each and every member of our staff, and I know that they will be a credit to both you and Mrs. McDuffie, as well as the Marsh family." She took a deep breath. "No, my worries are for His Majesty."

The butler frowned. "I hope the trip to America wasn't too much for His Majesty."

She shook her head. "No. The king is fine . . . well, apart from his heavy smoking. I just don't believe smoking is good for his health. No, my concern is something he said." She paused, and the butler waited. "Something isn't right, and he's worried. I could always tell when Bertie was worried about something, even as children." She smiled. "He wouldn't go into detail over the telephone, but something is not right." She gave the butler a sharp look. "I think we'd better keep our eyes and ears open. Something's afoot."

Chapter 6

The telephone rang several times before I remembered where I was and answered. "Hello."

I frowned when I recognized Delia Marshall's voice. My first instinct was to hang up. My second was to give her a piece of my mind and then hang up. Fortunately, Snickers woke up and stretched. One look at her face, and I knew I had to swallow my pride and the words that bounced around inside my head. I took a deep breath. "Hello, Delia. How are you feeling?"

"I don't . . . time for . . . need to talk . . . tonight . . ."

"Delia? You're breaking up. Can you repeat what you just said?"

"I'm about to reel in a big fish, and I don't have the time to waste with a small fry like you."

"Are you saying you aren't going to sue?" I held my breath.

"I have more important things to worry about right now."

"Delia . . . I don't know what to say. I'm—"

"Let's not pretend this is more than it is. This is business, nothing more. You've got something I need, and in exchange for that, I'll drop my lawsuit and let you keep your little dog."

I racked my brain to think what I had that would entice Delia to drop her suit, but nothing came to mind. "What do you want?"

"I want my book, *The Complete Works of Agatha Christie*. The one you ordered. You give me the book, tonight, and we're even. But it has to be tonight."

My brain was reeling. From what Jenna told me, I knew Delia could have asked for more, a lot more. In anyone else, I would have chalked it up to the goodness of their heart, but I was convinced Delia didn't have a heart. "Okay, sure. I'll get it to you right away." I glanced at the clock. "It's almost midnight. Are you sure you don't want to wait until tomorrow?"

"No. It has to be tonight. I'm about to bring in the motherload, and I need that book tonight."

I had a sick feeling in the pit of my stomach. Delia Marshall was about to extort money from someone else. Giving her that book made me feel like I was enabling her to hurt someone else. But, if I didn't, what would happen to my business? My book? Snickers?

"You get . . . book . . . meet . . . tonight." Our connection broke up again.

"Delia, you're breaking up again. Can you repeat—"

The connection ended.

I tried to redial, but the call immediately went to voicemail. I left a message and waited to see if Delia would call back. When she didn't, I decided to go to her house. I'd take the book, but maybe face-to-face I could reason with Delia. If not, I'd give her the book and deal with my guilty conscience later.

I headed down the hall, followed by Snickers and Oreo. I stopped by my second bedroom, but Nana Jo hadn't gotten home yet from her date with her boyfriend, Freddie. I glanced down at the poodles, who were stretching as if they'd had a rough day. "Given your history with Delia, I think you two had better stay here."

Snickers yawned as if to say, *I could care less.*

I let them outside and then gave them an extra treat before closing them in my bedroom and hurrying downstairs. I almost forgot the book, but I remembered at the last minute and hurried back to the bookstore to get it and lug it out to the car.

A couple of years ago, the *North Harbor Herald* featured an article about the big party Delia hosted at her South Harbor home. I'd never been invited, but I knew where it was.

In North Harbor's heyday, it had been the home of the wealthiest citizens. The wealth was reflected in the old Victorian homes that sat back from the cobblestone streets with vast lawns behind wrought-iron gates. Full of character and charm, North Harbor's mansions were a symbol of that former wealth. In contrast, South Harbor was populated with smaller, working-class bungalows. Delia Marshall lived on a street of 1950s bungalows. Hers was light blue with white trim.

I pulled into the driveway and took a few deep breaths before I got up the courage to get out. "I'm doing the right thing," I told myself, but no matter how many times I repeated the lie, I couldn't force myself to believe it.

The house was dark, and I hesitated before ringing the doorbell. *Is this the right house?* I glanced around and noticed the address plate included a picture of a raven along with her last name. It took a minute before I connected the dots and realized the raven was a reference to Edgar Allan Poe's famous story and the logo for an award offered by a prestigious mystery organization. *Duh, Edgar Allan Poe . . . of course she'd have a raven on her address plate. Poe is the father of the mystery genre, right?* Talking to myself was comforting. *Did she win a Raven?*

I couldn't remember. *Who knows?* I took a deep breath and rang the bell again. I waited. And waited. No lights came on, and there was an eerie silence that weighed on me like a blanket. After what felt like a few hours, but was mere seconds, I rang the bell again, but this time I followed it up with a knock. The door wasn't latched properly, and the door squeaked open. The hair on my arms stood up.

South Harbor locals flaunted their excellent schools and lower crime rates, but even South Harbor residents locked their doors at night, right? I stuck my face in the opening.

"Hello?"

Silence.

I took a deep breath and pushed the door open a bit more. "Delia, are you here? It's me, Samantha Washington."

I glanced around. None of the neighbors' lights had come on, which wasn't comforting. I looked for a sticker or sign that announced that Delia Marshall had some type of security system but found nothing. *Of course she doesn't have a security system. There's no crime in South Harbor.*

I pulled out my cell phone and debated calling the police. *What would I say? What am I doing here in the middle of the night? I'm bringing an expensive book to the woman who threatened to sue me as a payoff. That'll go over well.* I debated calling Frank, but he was out of town. He'd just worry about me and tell me to get in my car and go home. *I should get in my car and go home.* "I can't call Nana Jo. She's out on a date." I glanced at my watch. It was one in the morning. I refused to even contemplate what Jenna would say. *I should get in my car and drive home. Delia obviously isn't home, right? Then why did she call me and tell me to come and bring the book?* I paced on the small concrete porch. *What am I doing? It's the middle of the night. I don't even like Delia Marshall. I should go home and forget this whole thing.* I marched toward my car. I made it as far as the door. *She called me. She could be in there, hurt. I can't just walk away and leave her.* I glanced back at the house. *Ugh!* I turned around and stomped back to the porch.

I took a breath, pushed the door open, and took two steps inside. "Delia? Are you here?"

No response.

I swiped my cell and turned on the flashlight. I held it up and glanced around the living room.

The room was a wreck. Furniture tumbled over. Cushions strewn around the room. Papers covered the floor. I had no idea about Delia's normal cleaning habits, but this was clearly not normal.

I turned and ran to my car. Inside, I locked the doors. I started the engine but sat for a few seconds to allow my heart to stop racing and my hands to stop shaking. I put the car in reverse and backed up a few feet before I stopped. *I can't just leave. Delia could be injured. Crap. Do I call the police? And tell them what?* Eventually a lightbulb went off, and I picked up my phone and dialed.

A groggy voice answered. "You better have a really good reason for calling me at one o'clock in the morning," Detective Pitt mumbled.

I quickly explained where I was and that I suspected Delia Marshall might need help.

"Call the police."

"I am calling the police."

"I'm on medical leave recovering from a gunshot, in case you forgot. A gunshot I got saving your life."

I sighed. "I know, and I wouldn't call you except I'm really worried, and you're the only person I can trust." This wasn't true, but I'd found flattery went a long way with the North Harbor detective.

He sighed. "What's the address?"

I gave him the address. "Thank you, Detective. I don't know—"

"Yeah, yeah. Just stay in your car and don't touch anything." He hung up before I could say more.

I sat in the car in Delia Marshall's driveway and waited. Knowing someone knew where I was and was on their way helped calm my nerves a bit, even if that someone was Detective Bradley Pitt.

Geez. How sad is that? I can't believe I'm excited that Stinky Pitt is coming. I must really be desperate.

North Harbor Detective Bradley Pitt had been one of my grandmother's students in elementary school, where he'd picked up the unfortunate nickname of Stinky Pitt. I first encountered the detective when a body was found in the courtyard behind my bookstore. Then, Detective Pitt had been convinced that I was the killer. Since then, our paths had crossed a number of times. In fact, I'd actually helped solve several murders. Although Detective Pitt viewed my assistance as *meddling,* I liked to think we'd established a good relationship.

Headlights reflected in my rearview mirror as Detective Pitt's car pulled into the driveway. He parked so close that I couldn't open the driver's door.

Accident? His snide smile said no.

He got out of the car.

I rolled down my window. "Hey, I can't get out."

He motioned as if commanding a dog. "Stay."

I huffed and contemplated if I could climb over the center console of my Ford Escape to the passenger door.

Detective Pitt pulled out his gun and went to the front door. He knocked and announced himself. After a few moments, he entered.

I held my breath and stared at the door.

Eventually he walked out and came over to my car.

"Empty. Looks like someone trashed the house, but who's to say it wasn't like that to begin with."

"I doubt very seriously that Delia Marshall ripped her own furniture."

He shrugged. "Maybe. Maybe not. You say she called and asked you to come over?"

"Yes."

"Why?"

I hadn't shared the fact that Delia was planning to sue me and had instead resorted to extortion. "She asked me to bring her a book she'd ordered." I held up the book, but even to my own ears, my excuse sounded lame.

"In the middle of the night?"

"Well, it's a very valuable book, and she said she needed it."

He raised a brow, but when I didn't add anything, he sighed. "You're nosing around in something you shouldn't, but I'm going home. I left a note for Miss Marshall to call the North Harbor police, and I locked the door." He moved to get into his car.

"Is that it?"

"That's it."

"But what about Delia Marshall?"

"What about her? If you think she's missing, you can file a report with the North Harbor Police Department. Regardless, I'm going back to bed."

"But—"

Detective Pitt got into his car, turned on the engine, and backed out of the driveway.

I waited a few seconds but realized there wasn't anything else I could do. So, I backed out of the driveway and drove home.

It was after two when I got home. Exhausted, I didn't even have the strength to turn on the lights. I absolutely didn't have the strength to carry Delia's weighty book up a flight of stairs. So, I left it on a table.

Normally, Snickers and Oreo greet me when I come home, but they barely lifted their heads from their cushy positions in the middle of my bed.

I didn't bother moving them and flopped down on the sliver of bed space allotted for my use. I was used to the unfair distribution of the mattress and was asleep nearly as soon as my head hit the pillow.

"Sam. Wake up." Nana Jo shook my leg.

"Go away. I just lay down."

"Samantha Marie Washington, get up. NOW."

I forced my eyes open and turned my head to glare at my grandmother. "I was out late, and I just got here. I—"

"Sam, we have a problem."

"What? What is so important?"

"Delia Marshall is downstairs. She's—"

"She must have come for her book. It's downstairs somewhere. I don't want to talk to her." I turned over. "Can you just give it to her, please?"

"Sam, Delia Marshall's dead. Someone clubbed her to death with that book."

Chapter 7

Instantly, I was wide awake. I sat up. "You can't be serious."

Her silence and her face assured me she was.

"But how? How did she get in? When did she get in?"

She shrugged. "Beats me. I just got here."

"Who?" I couldn't get out the rest of the words, but Nana Jo didn't need them. She knew what I was asking.

"I have no idea, but I'm going to need a cup of coffee." She turned and headed toward the door. At the door, she turned back. "Come!"

Snickers and Oreo jumped off the bed and trotted after her.

I got up and crept downstairs to the bookshop.

On the floor in between the thriller and true crime sections lay Delia Marshall. She was flat on her face and had the leather-bound copy of *The Complete Works of Agatha Christie* on top of her head.

My stomach roiled. I hadn't liked Delia Marshall, but I didn't want her dead. I especially didn't want her dead here . . .

in my bookstore. That uncharitable thought spurred me to action. I went to my office at the back of the store, picked up the phone, and called the police.

When the 9-1-1 officer asked what my emergency was, I replied, "There's a dead woman in my bookstore."

Chapter 8

I dreaded my second call more than calling 9-1-1, but I sucked it up and dialed anyway.

"Jenna, I have a problem." I told my sister everything that happened from the moment Delia Marshall called me last night.

The kind, sympathetic person I talked to yesterday was gone. "Sam, what were you thinking driving over to that woman's house in the middle of the night . . . *by yourself*!" She took a breath and I tried to interject, but she wasn't listening. "Never mind, obviously you weren't thinking, or you never would have gone. Geez! And you took the murder weapon with you, so your fingerprints are all over it. How did she get in your building to begin with?"

By this point, I knew she didn't want me to answer that question. Right now, she needed to yell, so I held the phone and let her get it off her chest.

There was a knock at the door, which forced me to interrupt. "Jenna, the police are here, and I have to go. Are you coming?"

She sighed, and I didn't need to see her face to know she

was rolling her eyes. "I'll be there as soon as I get dressed. Don't say anything until I get there."

"But I have to—" It was too late. She'd already hung up.

Nana Jo opened the door and led the detectives to Delia's body. When I came out of the office, she was standing nearby holding Snickers and Oreo.

"I called Jenna. She's on her way."

She nodded. "I called *the girls*. They'll meet us at the café for lunch."

The girls were Nana Jo's friends from the Shady Acres Retirement Village.

Detective Pitt wasn't the sharpest knife in the drawer when it came to investigating a murder, but he was familiar. He was still out on medical leave and wouldn't be investigating Delia's murder.

"Do you think Chief Stevenson—"

Nana Jo was shaking her head before the words left my mouth. "Ruby Mae said he's in Washington at some law enforcement conference."

Nana Jo's friend Ruby Mae Stevenson's great-nephew was the acting chief of police. He was intelligent, open-minded, and fair. I was disappointed that he wouldn't be around to help. North Harbor's police force wasn't huge, and there weren't a lot of murders that would require a detective to hone their investigative skills. Domestic disputes and drunken brawls didn't require a great deal of thought or finesse.

"Who?"

Nana Jo shrugged. "Never seen either of these guys before. Must not be locals. I'd have recognized them if they grew up in North Harbor."

A detective walked back where we were standing.

He had a toothpick dangling out of the corner of his mouth. "You own this here . . . this . . ." He waved a hand around and frowned as though he was referring to a brothel.

"Bookstore? Yes." I extended my hand and forced a smile to hide the scowl I hadn't been able to stop. "My name's Samantha Washington. And you are?"

He looked at my hand as though I'd just finished spreading manure but reluctantly shook. "Detective Logan Fieldstone."

Detective Fieldstone was about five feet six with a smooth complexion and dark hair he wore in a buzz cut. He had on sunglasses that hid his eyes.

"What happened?" He spoke around the toothpick.

"I have no idea. My grandmother found the body. Maybe you should—"

"Miss Washington, I've heard about you. I've heard how you like to stick your nose in police business and play Nancy Drew, but I'm not Detective Pitt, and I don't need some rank amateur meddling on my investigation." He took his toothpick out of his mouth and pointed it at me. "So, you just answer my questions, or I'll run you in for interfering in an official police investigation. You got it?"

The Nancy Drew reference made my blood boil. And I could feel Nana Jo ready to pounce. Fortunately, we didn't have to.

Detective Fieldstone was so intent on his monologue that he didn't notice that Jenna had walked in and was standing behind him.

"And, if you ever threaten my client again, then I'll have you up before the police board so quickly, your head will spin, Detective." Jenna was only about five-four, but she stood so straight and tall, I would have sworn she was six feet tall. She scowled and managed to look down at him.

For a split second, I thought Detective Fieldstone was going to be stupid enough to challenge my sister when she was in full-blown mama-bear-if-you-mess-with-my-family-I'll-rip-your-face-off mode. But Detective Fieldstone came to his senses and stepped back.

I released the breath I'd been holding.

"Your client?" He glanced from me to Jenna and smirked. "Now, why would you think you need to call an attorney, Miss Washington?"

I opened my mouth but closed it as I saw my sister's jaw tighten.

"Because *Mrs.* Washington isn't a fool. She knows her rights. She also knows that she would be a fool to talk to the police without legal counsel present to make sure that her rights are respected and that she isn't bullied or threatened."

A vein on the side of Detective Fieldstone's head pulsed, and his jaw was so tight he looked as though he could spit nails.

Another detective walked up behind Detective Fieldstone. "Ah, Counselor Rutherford. I didn't know you were involved in this."

Jenna pulled her gaze away from Detective Fieldstone. "Detective Montgomery Deevers, they have you training the rookie?"

While Detective Fieldstone would have been considered a lightweight, Detective Deevers was definitely in the heavyweight division. Five feet ten and about two-eighty, he looked about the same fighting class as Nana Jo. Although, if the two ever did find themselves in a match, my money was on my grandmother.

Deevers was muscular, with light blue eyes, a square jaw, and the same buzz cut as his partner.

"Detective Fieldstone doesn't need me. He graduated at the top of his class. He's a good cop and eager to do his job. Now, I'm sure he didn't mean any disrespect to your *sister* or your *grandmother*." He grinned. "Maybe we can go into your office and sit down and get comfortable and start this all over."

I led the way into my office, and Detective Deevers waited while Nana Jo, Jenna, and I sat down. Then, he hurried into the conference room where the Mystery Mavens had met yesterday and grabbed chairs for him and his partner. Gawd, was it only yesterday that all of this craziness began?

"Detective Fieldstone, are you having a problem with the light?" Jenna asked. "It's three thirty in the morning, and you're wearing sunglasses inside."

The vein on the side of the detective's head went into overdrive, and I was concerned that an alien might leap out. However, the detective reached up, removed his glasses, and glared.

The tension in the room felt like a corset choking the breath out of me.

"Would anyone like coffee?" Nana Jo asked.

Deevers nodded. Jenna and Detective Fieldstone were still glaring at each other like prizefighters sizing each other up at the start of a match.

"I'll help you." I hopped up and forced myself not to run from the room.

Nana Jo and I came back, and each of us carried two Styrofoam cups with steam coming up. Knowing my sister as I did, one of my cups had hot water and an English breakfast tea bag. I handed her the cup, reached in my pocket, and pulled out two packets of raw sugar before sitting down with my own cup.

Once we were all seated, Detective Deevers pulled out a notepad and waited.

Nana Jo and I exchanged a glance, and then she shrugged. "I'll go first. My name's Josephine Thomas. I found Delia Marshall lying here on the floor when I came home from my date."

Deevers made a production of glancing at his watch. He smiled and then winked at Nana Jo. "Anyone who can corroborate that?"

She gave the name of her boyfriend.

"Would that be ex-North Harbor police detective Freddie Williams? Father of Michigan state policeman Trooper Mark Williams?"

"That's the one," Nana Jo said.

A brief glance passed between Deevers and Fieldstone. Detective Deevers grinned at Nana Jo. "Well, I don't think you could have a better alibi than that." He turned his glance to me. "Now, *Mrs. Washington*, may I call you Samantha?"

I nodded.

"Good. Now, why don't you tell me what happened?"

"I don't know. I was upstairs writing when I got a call from Delia saying she wanted to meet with me." One thing I learned from working with the police was to answer their questions, but not to volunteer information. So, I stuck to the facts.

"What time was this?" Deevers asked.

"Just before midnight."

He whistled. "That's rather late for a call. You two must have been pretty close for her to call that late at night."

His tone was jovial and friendly . . . too friendly.

I glanced at Jenna, whose gaze conveyed caution without saying a word.

"I just met Delia Marshall two days ago." I explained how I volunteered to help the North Harbor Library by allowing some of their book clubs to meet here after the tornadoes.

I explained that the connection was bad, and I assumed Delia wanted me to bring her the book, so I'd gone to her home. He'd find out about my visit to her house soon enough, so I might as well get it on the table early.

Detective Deevers asked quite a few questions and said he'd follow up with Detective Pitt later.

I finished recounting my actions. Detective Fieldstone sat tight-lipped and quiet when he wasn't glaring at Jenna.

"Now, I just want to get this down right," Deevers said.

"You're saying that Delia Marshall wasn't lying on the floor dead when you got home and went upstairs?" Innocence dripped from his words.

"I'm saying that I was tired. The lights were out, and it was dark. I don't think she was here. I don't see how—"

"You don't see how what?" Deevers's eyes sparkled. He leaned forward. For a brief moment, his mask dropped, and I saw the real detective. "You don't see how you could have missed her if she had been killed by someone else and lying on the floor because you would have had to step over her to get upstairs? Or how she could have gotten into a building that was locked with a security system unless you or someone who knew the code to disarm it had let her in? Or how she could have been beaten to death with a book that you admit to having in your possession in the presence of a police officer earlier in the night?"

Detective Fieldstone smirked.

Jenna stood up. "Detective Deevers, my sister did NOT murder Delia Marshall. And it's not her job to figure out how or why Ms. Marshall was murdered. That's your job. You've got her statement. Unless you're prepared to charge my sister or my grandmother with murder, we're done."

"We're just trying to get to the heart of the situation." Deevers, mask back in place, smiled. But it was too late. We'd seen his true nature, and he knew he'd shown his hand. His nice guy routine wouldn't work.

He and Detective Fieldstone left, but not until they promised to return later. Or was it a threat?

They walked out, and Jenna slammed the door behind them.

I didn't realize I was shaking until Nana Jo wrapped her arms around me and hugged me.

"It'll be okay, Sam. We know you didn't murder that woman."

"But who could have done it? And how did they get in?" I pulled back and stared at my grandmother. "Was the door open when you came home? Maybe I forgot to turn the security system on after I got home?"

Nana Jo frowned. "The alarm was definitely *not* turned on, but . . . the back door was locked. I remember fumbling with my keys to unlock it when I got home."

"Where did you leave the book when you came home?" Jenna asked.

I searched my brain to remember. "I think I just left it on the shelf. It was so heavy, I didn't want to lug it up a flight of stairs, only to have to turn around and bring it back down in a few hours."

Jenna sat down and pulled out a tape recorder. "Now, I want you to tell me *everything* that happened from the moment Delia Marshall stepped foot in here two days ago."

I sat down and related everything.

Jenna asked a few clarifying questions, but she just let me talk for the most part. Nana Jo filled in a few things, but it was mostly me trying to remember everything I could. When I was so tired I could barely remember my name, she turned off the recorder.

"It's bad, isn't it?" I asked.

Jenna hesitated a few seconds. "I'm not going to lie. It's bad. I would be shocked if they don't come back with a warrant for your arrest later today or tomorrow at the latest."

"I can't believe this is happening. What's going to happen to my bookstore? Snickers and Oreo? My publisher will probably cancel my book. They're not going to want a jailbird for a client." I put my head in my hands.

"This is no time to fall apart," Nana Jo said.

"Oh, I don't know, it seems like a pretty good time to me," I mumbled through my hands.

"Now, you listen to me. If we're going to figure out who

murdered Delia Marshall, and by *we* I mean you, then you're going to need to have your wits about you. So, buck up and keep it together." Nana Jo said that last command like a drill sergeant.

I glanced between my fingers. "I can't figure out who killed Delia Marshall. My brain is mush, and I'm an emotional basket case."

"Sam, I hate to say it, but Nana Jo's right," Jenna said. "I'll do what I can, but it doesn't look good. You had a motive. You had the opportunity. And you had the means." She counted them off on her fingers as she talked. She paused and let the gravity of her words sink in before she added, "If you don't snap out of it and get your brain working, then things are going to be very bad."

Chapter 9

By the time I maneuvered around the multitude of people who were working in the bookstore and made my way upstairs, my head felt like a drum in a marching band. I could feel the blood pulsing and was afraid I'd have a stroke. So, I took a couple of aspirin, turned off the lights, and lay down on the bed.

I wasn't surprised when I couldn't sleep. I picked up my phone and started a call to Frank but hung up before pressing SEND. There wasn't anything he could do. He'd left to visit his mother. He'd invited me to go, but I wasn't ready to meet my fiancé's mother . . . not yet. We'd talked on the phone a few times, and Dr. Camilia Patterson had been nice. She said all the right words about how happy she was that her son had finally found a woman he wanted to share his life with, but there was something in her tone that said she was disappointed in the choice he'd made. I knew from Frank that she was highly respected in her field and that she sat on the boards of various nonprofits. She was a philanthropist and extremely well respected. If she found out her son was going to marry someone about to be arrested for murder, she'd lose her cool.

And do what? Forbid Frank from marrying me? That wouldn't work. Frank was an adult. He'd never allow his mother or anyone else to dictate his life. As someone who spent years in the military involved in top-secret things for the government, Frank Patterson was his own man. Then why was I hesitating? I glanced over at Snickers, who was curled up asleep on my pillow. Her muzzle was only inches from my face. Her eyes flickered, and she stared at me as though she'd heard my thoughts.

I stared back. "I can't call him because when I'm arrested, then his mother will know that she was right. I'm not good enough for her son."

Snickers sniffed, stood up, and turned around three times before lying down again. This time, her back was to me.

The pounding subsided a bit, but my brain wouldn't stop. I couldn't listen to my thoughts anymore and got up and went over to my desk. A bit of time in the British countryside always helped to calm my thoughts.

King George VI stood in front of the large bay window that took up an entire wall in the king's drawing room of Windsor Castle. His window offered an excellent view of Eton across the River Thames. The massive, ornately formal room had an elaborate plaster ceiling decorated with the coat of arms of his grandfather, George IV, and the Garter Star. The walls were hung with fabric featuring a repeating motif of the royal coat of arms surrounded by the garter and collar of the Order of the Garter, all surmounted by a crown and edged with leaves. On the floor was a Wilton carpet with a strong geometric design. At the bay end of the room, a circular table atop legs shaped in a lion's head and feet sat on a Persian-style carpet.

Lord James Browning walked around the room admiring the paintings, almost all of which were by the Flemish master Sir Peter Paul Rubens. "I can see why they called this the Reubens Room."

"My grandmother always loved paintings from the Flemish school," Lady Elizabeth said. "She especially loved that one." She pointed to the large painting that hung over the fireplace. *The Holy Family with St. Francis.*"

A haze of smoke drifted up around the king's head. He coughed and then turned to face his guest. "I'm grateful you were able to adjust your plans."

"Of course. We were honored, but . . ." Lady Elizabeth hesitated.

King George grinned. "But you're wondering why?"

Lady Elizabeth waited.

King George paced and smoked. Eventually, he paused, took a deep breath. "I asked you to come because I need your help."

Lady Elizabeth nodded. "I thought as much. Now, Bertie, sit down and tell me what's happened."

King George VI, Albert Frederick, Arthur George, Bertie to his family, smiled at his cousin. Seated, the king finished his cigarette. When he was done, he took a deep breath, resulting in a coughing fit. When he was able to speak, he said, "There's been a murder."

"I was afraid of that. If you want my help, I'll need to know all of the details."

There was a brief knock on the door. Godfrey, a short, mature butler who had been with the royal family for many years, entered and pushed a cart toward the table where Lady Elizabeth and the king sat.

"Shall I play mother?" Lady Elizabeth asked. After receiving a brief nod from the king, she began to pour.

As Godfrey bowed and turned to leave, Lady Elizabeth said, "Godfrey, would you please ask Thompkins to join us?"

"Yes, your ladyship." He gave a brief bow and left.

Lady Elizabeth poured the tea.

There was a brief knock, and then the door was opened. Thompkins took two steps into the drawing room, bowed deeply to the king, and then turned to face Lady Elizabeth.

"Thompkins, there's been a murder. I'd like you to stay and hear this." She turned to the king, who nodded briefly, before she returned her gaze to the butler. "I don't think we'll have a great deal of time, so I'll need you to get busy finding out what you can from the servants."

The butler nodded and moved back to the wall where he stood as still as a statue.

"Now, please tell us as much as you can," Lady Elizabeth said.

The king sipped his tea, leaned back in his chair, and took a deep breath. "Milicent Schmidt. That's her name. She was a correspondent with the *London Times.*"

"Did you know her before she came?" Lady Elizabeth asked. The question was innocent, but there was something in her tone that brought a smile to the king's lips.

"Never seen her before in my life."

"I'm sorry, but I had to ask." Lady Elizabeth reached out and squeezed her cousin's hand and smiled.

Lord James Browning sat on a long sofa near the fireplace. The duke, who had been quiet up to that point, put his teacup down, lit a pipe, and crossed his leg. "What about the duke? Did he know her?"

The king lit another cigarette and took several drags before responding. "I don't believe he did, but who knows. David never was very discerning where women were concerned." He shook his head. "As we can see from his current situation."

Despite his words, Lady Elizabeth knew that Albert loved his brother, David. The two had once been close, but the strain of his elder brother's abdication to marry the twice-divorced American, Wallis Simpson, had caused a breach she feared the two would never mend. "Go on," Lady Elizabeth said quietly.

"She was supposed to be doing a story about the Commonwealth and Britain's role in the world order as the country prepares for war. The navy, Britannia rules the waves . . . you know the type of thing." He puffed on his cigarette. "I hate interviews, but the ministry thought it would be good publicity. It would help the country prepare for war."

"So, war is coming?"

The king nodded.

"How long?"

"Not more than a few months. If the reports are accurate."

Lord Browning rose. "They are. The Nazis are mobilizing their forces. We believe he's planning to invade Poland before the end of the year."

Lord James Browning, 15th Duke of Kingsfordshire, was not only a British aristocrat, but he was also a member of Britain's secret service. Fair-haired and freckled, James had a fresh face and broad shoulders. He looked like someone who'd be comfortable on a football pitch or sitting astride a horse preparing to go to hounds rather than a spy, which was exactly the reason he'd been so successful.

"If the Nazis invade Poland, Britain and France will come to her aid." He turned to the king. "Will the Americans help?"

The king smoked for several moments. Eventually, he shrugged. "I don't know. Roosevelt got elected by promising that America wouldn't enter another war in Europe. He understands how dangerous Hitler is, but . . . I don't know. He's promised to do what he can, but we may be on our own unless something happens to force his hand."

"Surely, he has to know that Hitler and the Nazis won't stop with Europe," Lady Elizabeth said. "It's just a matter of time before he'll look to destroy them, too."

"I'm sure he does. However, things are complicated. He's just bringing his country out of a depression and another war might give his political opponents the leverage needed to undo all that he's done. Plus, he's not well. I don't even know if the American people know how ill he really is." King George took a deep breath. "Like I said, it's complicated. Anyway, Milicent Schmidt came to Windsor. She interviewed a few people. However, a few days ago, I received a note." He pulled an envelope from his pocket and handed it to his cousin.

"Meet me at St. George's Chapel at midnight, or my next story in the *Times* will be the one that puts an end to the House of Windsor's (or should I say, Saxe-Coburg-Gotha's) grip on the throne of England," Lady Elizabeth read and then passed the note to Lord Browning.

Lord Browning read the note and examined the envelope. "No postal code."

"Surely you didn't go?" Lady Elizabeth asked. The king's silence answered her question. She closed her eyes. "You met her, and then what happened?"

"Nothing. She was dead when I arrived." King George rose and walked back to the bay window. "When she was rolled over, several documents from my red box were found under her body."

Lord Browning gasped. "Dear God."

Lady Elizabeth looked from Lord Browning to her cousin. "Red box?"

King George lit another cigarette and inhaled deeply and then walked to his desk, opened a drawer, and pulled out a red dispatch box. "Every day, except Christmas and Easter, a dispatch is delivered in a red box. They contain important documents from Parliament and other Commonwealth countries. Anything that requires my signature is delivered in one of these red boxes."

"And given the current state of affairs, I take it there's information that would be dangerous if it made it into the wrong hands," Lady Elizabeth said.

The king nodded.

"You said documents were found under her body," Lord Browning said. "Is anything missing?"

"Th-th-thankfully, no, but th-th-at doesn't mean the information c-c-couldn't have been duplicated and passed along." The king ran a hand through his hair and puffed on his cigarette.

The king's boyhood stammer had become more prominent, indicative of his heightened sense of anxiety.

"How could this happen?" Lord Browning asked. "The box was locked, right?"

"Of c-c-ourse it was." He reached into his pocket and pulled out a key. "And I've got the k-k-key."

"Is there another key?" Lady Elizabeth asked.

The king shook his head.

Lady Elizabeth stared at her cousin. He was agitated, but she could tell he was holding back.

"I understand that the documents were taken from your red box, but you've recovered them, so nothing is exactly missing, correct?" she asked.

The king nodded.

"Well, the fact that someone managed to take them in the first place has to be distressing, but I can't help but feel that you're holding back," Lady Elizabeth said. "Bertie, if you want our help, you've got to trust us and tell us everything."

The king stood in silence for several moments. Eventually, he reached into his pocket and pulled out a small piece of lace. He walked to his cousin and handed it to her.

Lady Elizabeth stared at the material.

The king's face looked tortured. Eventually, he said, "She had that clutched in her hand when I found her. I recognized it at once." He paused. "It's from a shawl that was given as a gift . . . to my mother. She'd been wearing the shawl earlier that night, and it wasn't torn."

Lord Browning groaned. "That means the queen mother was one of the last people to see Milicent Schmidt alive."

"You'll never convince me that my mother k-k-killed that woman. But it looks bad. That's why we need you." King George faced his cousin. "If the police or the press find out about this, they'll c-c-crucify her. They'll think M-M-Milicent knew something about me, or more likely D-D-David, that could ruin our family. It certainly doesn't help that David and Mrs. S-S-Simpson have been c-c-corresponding with Hitler and Ribbentrop." He ran his hand through his hair. "I need you to find the real killer. B-Br-Britain is standing on the brink of war, and the House of Windsor can't withstand another scandal. P-Pl-Please, I need you . . . B-Br-Britain needs you."

Lady Elizabeth faced her cousin and nodded. "Of course. I'll do everything I can for you and for Britain."

Chapter 10

Writing always made me feel better. Nana Jo said when I wrote, my subconscious mind was able to process the things going on in my real world and helped me figure out who-dunit. I wasn't sure about the science behind her theory. However, I did feel better. My headache had moved down a few notches. One of the reasons I'd chosen to set my British historical mystery in Great Britain at the start of World War II was because of my admiration of the grit of the British. Most of the world, still reeling from the devastation of World War I, turned a blind eye to Germany's rearmament and annexation of Austria and Czechoslovakia. Yet, despite a concerted effort to "appease" Hitler rather than confront him, there were scores of men and women who put their lives on the line to stand up for what was right. It was that resolve that sparked me to stop wallowing in self-pity and help myself. I needed to figure out who killed Delia Marshall, and I wasn't going to do it lying in bed waiting for Detectives Fieldstone and Deevers to arrest me.

I glanced at my watch, but my stomach told me it was time for lunch.

I opened the door to my bedroom and nearly ran into Nana Jo, who was standing outside my door, hand raised to knock. "I'm starving."

Nana Jo raised an eyebrow. "Good. Let's go get some food and get this investigation underway."

I let Snickers and Oreo out to take care of business and then gave them a snack and left them to devour it in the privacy and comfort of my bedroom, while Nana Jo and I headed downstairs.

The police mob was gone, but the devastation they had left in their wake would have brought tears to my eyes if I'd had any left to shed. The books, papers, and chairs they'd rearranged would be easy to set right. The powder from fingerprints was another story, but Market Street Mysteries was closed until further notice, so I would worry about cleaning that later.

Nana Jo and I walked the short distance to the North Harbor Café. When we arrived, the hostess smiled and pointed upstairs.

Unlike my building, the upper floor of Frank's hadn't been converted into residential space. He had plans to rid the space of its 1970s décor, with hideous gold foil and flocked wallpaper and geometric-patterned carpeting. But it wasn't a priority. He only used the space for overflow. And I wasn't complaining.

There was a large, long rectangular table, and the girls were already seated when we arrived.

Nana Jo took her seat at the head of the table, and I sat at the empty chair to her right.

Our server was a young girl named Morgan with purple hair that was shaved on one side and gelled into spikes on the other, a tattoo sleeve that depicted characters from the Chronicles of Narnia, and too many piercings to count. She hurried to my side. "Hey, Mrs. W. Wanna see my new tat?"

"Absolutely." I smiled as she pulled back the neck of her white blouse, which was part of her uniform, and showed me a bright orange tiger on her shoulder. "Is that Tigger from *Winnie-the-Pooh*?"

"Yep. I love Tigger." Morgan beamed.

"I love your eclectic literary taste."

She scribbled down my beverage order. "I'm going to save room for one of your characters just as soon as your book's released." She winked and then hurried off to get our drinks.

Nana Jo leaned over. "Which one do you think will end up on her butt? Lady Elizabeth? Or Thompkins?"

I swatted Nana Jo's arm. "Shh. I think it's sweet."

"I'm not opposed to tattoos. I have one myself, but—"

"Wait." I stared at my grandmother. "You have a tattoo?"

"Of course. I wasn't always an old woman. But she needs to be careful because as you age, what starts out on her shoulder could end up shifting, and that isn't pretty."

Wow! Mid-thirties, and I never knew my grandmother had a tattoo. That meant it had to be in an area that isn't easily visible. I tried to keep my mind from wondering where, but it wouldn't comply.

We waited until Morgan returned with our beverages and finished taking our food orders before starting.

Nana Jo pulled out her iPad to signal it was time to get down to business. "All right, we don't have a lot of time, so let's get this show on the road."

Nana Jo summarized the situation, which sounded even more bleak spoken out loud than it did in my head.

Silence descended like a weight and sucked the air out of the room.

"Sounds like you need all the help you can get."

I turned to see who spoke and locked eyes with Detective Pitt. He stood at the top of the stairs.

Detective Bradley Pitt was short, barely taller than my five feet four inches. He wore polyester that was too short and too tight. He was bald, and what few hairs remained on top of his head were combed over to cover his dome. He'd gotten shot saving my life and lost a lot of weight while he recovered, so while his wardrobe was still mired in polyester, it was fitting a bit looser than it had a few months ago.

"Is this a private party?" Detective Pitt said.

"It is a private party." I stopped and walked over to the detective and gave him a big hug. "But you're very welcome."

Nana Jo wiped the smile from her face. "Sit down, Detective. I never thought I'd be saying this, but we're glad you're here."

The group skootched down and made room for another chair. Detective Pitt sat down next to Jenna, who sat on Nana Jo's left.

Detective Pitt and I didn't always see eye to eye. He'd been wrong when he accused me, Nana Jo, my stepfather, and my assistant, Dawson Alexander, of murder. In fact, we rarely agreed on much of anything, but something about his being there reassured me.

"I've already called Geoff," Ruby Mae Stevenson said. "He's going to take me to dinner, and I'll find out everything I can."

In her mid-sixties, Ruby Mae was the youngest of Nana Jo's friends, and though I'd never admit it publicly, she was my favorite. She was a Black woman with salt-and-pepper hair that she always wore pulled back in a bun. With nine children and a vast number of grandchildren, nieces, nephews, and greats, she had the largest extended family I'd ever seen. Everywhere we went, we ran into one of her relatives. Originally from Alabama, she spoke with a Southern drawl, which she never lost even after spending more than two-thirds of her life in the Midwest. She claimed knitting helped her think, and she was always knitting something, which is probably where I got the idea for Lady Elizabeth's penchant for knitting in my books.

"Great," Nana Jo said. She updated her iPad.

"I should have more to report by tomorrow morning, but he did say that Delia Marshall was a blackmailer," Ruby Mae said. "In fact, she tried to blackmail him."

While I knew what Delia had tried with me, I still found it shocking to hear that I wasn't her only victim.

Irma Starczewski glanced at her watch. "I've got a date with Bernie Goldberg later tonight. We're going to dinner."

"Who's Bernie Goldberg?" Nana Jo asked.

"Bernie's the largest real estate developer in North Harbor. He's got a finger in everything."

"What does Bernie have to do with Delia Marshall?"

"I hadn't heard she was involved in real estate," I said, still confused but looking for a tie-in between Delia and Bernie.

Irma shrugged. "I don't know if Delia Marshall was involved in real estate or not. But, my great-grandson, Ernie, is a Realtor. And when I told him where Delia Marshall lived, he told me to talk to Bernie."

The room was quiet for a split second, but Nana Jo broke the silence. "I may regret asking this, but *why* did Ernie think you should talk to Bernie Goldberg?"

Irma pulled a flask from her purse and took a sip before answering. "Because Bernie Goldberg owned the house where Delia Marshall lived. In fact, he owned the entire neighborhood."

Nana Jo narrowed her eyes and mumbled something that sounded like *dingbat*.

"Thank you, Irma," I said, flashing her an encouraging smile. "I never thought of looking into her landlord. That was very smart."

Irma pulled a compact from her purse and powdered her nose. "I might have to work on him all night, but I'll have something by tomorrow morning."

Irma Starczewski was the oldest of Nana Jo's friends. Barely five feet tall and one hundred pounds, Irma wore her hair in a beehive. She drank like a fish, cursed like a sailor, and was, according to my grandmother, a nymphomaniac. All of that was true. It was also true that Irma had a heart as big as Lake Michigan.

Nana Jo rolled her eyes but updated her iPad.

"I'm going to a reading by Denver Benedict this afternoon," Dorothy Clark added.

"I didn't know you knew Denver Benedict," Nana Jo said.

"According to my granddaughter, Jillian, he's been working on turning his award-winning novel into a stage play. Jillian's put the word around with the right people in the arts that I might be interested in investing. Jillian is confident he'll try to schmooze me to convince me to invest."

Of all my grandmother's friends, Dorothy Clark was the one who was most like my Nana Jo. At six feet tall, three hundred pounds, and in her mid-seventies, Dorothy most resembled Nana Jo in appearance. Both Dorothy and Nana Jo were also aikido experts. Despite the fact that Dorothy looked like a linebacker, she loved to flirt and had a deep sultry voice that she used to her advantage. She'd get information out of Denver Benedict one way or another.

Jenna took a long sip of her tea and then looked at me. "I talked to the district attorney. Based on the preliminary information, it looks likely that you'll be arrested."

My heart raced, and I had to take several deep breaths before I could speak. "I understand."

"He owes me a favor, so he is going to let me know in advance so you can voluntarily surrender. I'm working on bail, and . . ." She glanced down.

"What?"

"I called Harold."

I was shocked, but my face must have said what my vocal cords couldn't because she held up her hands.

"I'm sorry, but I felt it was the right thing to do. She's your mother. She has a right to know, and she'd be so hurt if we didn't tell her."

"She's your mother, too. And you know how she is. I can't believe—"

Nana Jo held up her hands to stop our fight. "Jenna's right."

"What? You're taking her side?"

"I'm not taking anyone's side. This isn't about sides. It's about doing the right thing. Grace is your mother. She deserves to know what's going on. Besides, she's halfway around the world in Australia."

I loved my mother, but she wasn't the person I'd go to in a crisis. I glared across the table at my sister, but Jenna shook it off.

"I told Harold, not Mom." Jenna shrugged. "He's offered to wire whatever amount is needed for bail. If we're even able to get bail. Usually, the DA doesn't allow for bail, but I think he will in this case." She took a deep breath. "Plus, Harold will break the news to Mom and do what he can to keep her calm."

My stepfather, Harold Robertson, had been a rocket scientist. He was also the heir to a department store and was the wealthiest person I knew. He was generous to a fault and loved my mother with his entire heart. If anyone was able to keep my mother calm, it was Harold. I just hoped he'd keep her in Australia. The last thing I needed while trying to prove my innocence was to have to deal with my mother in the middle of hysterics. She would consider this entire thing as an ordeal meant to wreak havoc on her nerves.

"Fine," I mumbled.

"The district attorney also suggested that I talk to Preston Kincaid."

"Preston Kincaid? Why does that name sound familiar?"

"Because it was plastered all over the newspapers a few years ago," Detective Pitt said.

Nana Jo snapped her fingers. "I remember now. He was a politician or wannabe politician. You can always tell when those guys start ramping up to make a political move. They can't sneeze without holding a press conference first. One minute, he's all over the papers and then he just dropped off the radar."

Detective Pitt nodded. "He was flying high, until he had a run-in with Delia Marshall."

"Wow." I stared from Detective Pitt to my sister. "What happened?"

Jenna shrugged. "I know Delia Marshall ruined his career, but I don't know the details. I'm going to talk to him later tonight. I doubt that he's going to confess to murder, but I'm hoping he can give me some insight into how she worked and maybe some names of other people who may have wanted her dead."

"That leaves Martha Chiswick and Evelyn Randolph," Nana Jo said.

"Why don't you take Martha, and I'll talk to Evelyn," I said. "Or we can talk to them together."

"That works for me," Nana Jo said. "Is that okay with everyone?"

Detective Pitt frowned. "What about me?"

"I was hoping you could get us a bit of information from the coroner's office," I said. "Was Delia really killed with *The Complete Works of Agatha Christie*? Along with any other forensic information found at the scene. Whose fingerprints did they find on the book and in the bookstore?"

Detective Pitt nodded.

"Great," Nana Jo said. "Is that it?"

"Not quite."

I turned to the stairs and saw Frank Patterson staring at me. And he didn't look happy.

Chapter 11

Walking down the stairs so Frank and I could talk privately, I felt like a kid who'd just been summoned to the principal's office.

Frank had carved out a tiny space at the back end of the kitchen that he used as an office. The room held a small table that he used for a desk, and a chair. There was a door, but the walls didn't go all the way to the ceiling, so anyone in the kitchen would be able to hear if he yelled. In all of the time I'd known Frank, I'd never heard him yell, and I hoped this wasn't going to be the first time.

He waited for me to enter before closing the door. He stood with his hands on his hips and scowled down at me. "Well?"

I looked around that tiny room, searching for something to latch onto. I looked everywhere except into Frank's soft brown eyes. There was a lot that I didn't know about Frank's life before we met, especially when it came to the work he'd done for the government. Most of it was classified. I knew he spoke a number of different languages and that he knew ways to kill silently and had contacts that could get information that the president of the United States probably couldn't get. But I also knew that he truly loved me. I decided to go with that.

I flung myself into his arms and held on to him as tightly as I could. Apparently, I wasn't as bereft of tears as I had been earlier because within seconds, Frank's shirt was soaked.

He wrapped his arms around me and held me close and tight until the tears stopped.

I glanced up at him. "How did you find out? Is it in the newspapers already?"

He rested his chin on my head. "Not yet."

"Then how did you . . ." I looked up at him and saw an expression that told me not to ask questions that he couldn't answer.

"Are you able to talk?" Frank asked.

I hiccupped and nodded.

He opened the door and stepped outside. He was back within seconds and handed me a clean white napkin and a bottle of water.

I sat in the one and only chair, wiped my face with the handkerchief, took a sip of water, and rehashed the nightmare of my encounters with Delia Marshall, while he leaned against the wall and listened.

"Jenna says I'll probably be arrested soon."

"You've got time, but not much. We need to figure out what Delia Marshall was up to and find her killer."

Something in his face made me suspicious. "How do you know I've got time?"

He pulled me into a hug. "You know better than to ask questions I can't answer. Let's just say I know people."

"What people?"

He kissed me. "Let's just say I know someone who bought us a little time. It's not much. We've only got about a week. So, you'd better get those little gray cells fired up. You've got to find a killer."

Chapter 12

"Now, what do you want me to do?" Frank asked.

Knowing I had the love and support of my friends and family warmed my heart. Having Frank here brought a smile to my face. "I was hoping that you could use some of your contacts to find out who Delia Marshall talked to last night." I thought for a few seconds. "Maybe for the last month. And perhaps . . . bank statements? If she tried blackmail with me, then she probably tried it with others. It would be great if we could find out who was paying her off."

"Done."

I smiled. "Do I want to know how you're going to get that information?"

"Nope. Let's just say I know somebody."

I worked up my courage and asked, "What did your mother say when you had to leave so suddenly? I'll bet that conversation was one you never thought you'd have to have. 'Sorry, Mom. I've got to go. My fiancée is about to be arrested for murder.'"

"I have no idea what she said or thinks. It's none of her business. I told her something came up and I had to leave."

He looked down at me. "But it wouldn't matter to me if she did know. I love you, and that's all that matters."

I felt weepy again, so I snuggled closer. "You know I love you, right?"

Even though I wasn't looking at him, I could feel the smile rise inside him. "Yep. But you should have called me. I shouldn't have to find out from . . . well, from others that you're in trouble."

"I know. And I promise that if I'm ever in danger of being arrested again, you'll be the first person I call."

After a few minutes of reconnecting, we decided to rejoin the others upstairs.

By the time we returned, everyone else had finished eating and was leaving.

Frank and I were going to eat together, but a kitchen emergency sent him hurrying back downstairs to sort things out.

Nana Jo was one of the last to leave. "I was going to ask if you and Frank got things worked out, but I can tell by the grin on your face and the sparkle in your eyes that you did."

Morgan handed me a bag. Frank had my food remade and packaged to go.

I smiled. Food was how he expressed his love, and I was grateful to be the recipient.

When I got home and opened the bag, I wasn't surprised to find he'd added several slices of cake. I was about to dive into the caramel cake when I had a thought.

I closed the Styrofoam lid and picked up my phone. The librarian had given me a list of names and telephone numbers for the Mystery Mavens, so I found the e-mail. I glanced at Snickers, who was sitting by my feet waiting for me to drop my lunch. She'd long ago established that anything that hit the floor belonged to her. I glanced at her eager face. "Sorry, girl. I have other plans for this cake."

She must have understood me because she sniffed, turned, and walked away.

Oreo didn't give up quite that quickly, and he stayed nearby, eyes glued to my bag.

I took a deep breath and dialed Evelyn Randolph before I could talk myself out of calling. "Evelyn, this is Samantha Washington from Market Street Mysteries. I'm terribly sorry to hear about Delia. I hope it won't seem insensitive, but with your new book out, I know how important early book sales are, and I was hoping you were still willing to sign some of my stock and nail down a date and time for a reading."

Evelyn was enthusiastic and eager. She said she could be here in thirty minutes, which worked out great.

I hung up and glanced over at Nana Jo, who gave me a thumbs-up.

"Do you want me to call Martha?" she asked.

"No, I'll do it." I already had the Mystery Mavens' telephone numbers easily available, so I quickly called.

Martha Chiswick was just as eager as Evelyn and promised to be here in an hour.

I hung up. "I think Evelyn is the weaker of the two. Maybe we can get her to talk before Martha arrives."

That was my plan anyway.

The police had taped off the bookstore, so they would have to enter from the side door by the parking lot. I waited downstairs in my office.

Good news travels fast and bad news travels at the speed of light, especially in a small town like North Harbor. News of Delia Marshall's murder would be making its rounds, and I wasn't looking forward to the media coverage. North Harbor may not have been a mecca for the media, but Delia Marshall had a syndicated column. Her murder was bound to attract attention.

I wasn't expecting visitors. When the doorbell rang, I hurried to the door, barely glancing out the window, confident that the face in the glass would be Evelyn Randolph. So, when I glanced out, I nearly did a double take. I stared for a few seconds and then fumbled to open the door. "Evelyn?"

Evelyn Randolph hesitated. "You still wanted me to sign books, right?"

"Umm, yes. I'm sorry. I just . . . yes . . . please come in." I stepped back and used my foot to keep Oreo from pouncing on her.

I made a conscientious effort to stop staring, but it was hard. Dowdy, drab Evelyn Randolph had undergone a metamorphosis. Overnight, she'd transformed herself from a caterpillar to a butterfly. Today, her mousy brown hair was cut short and highlighted with soft curls that framed her face and brought out the flecks of gold in her eyes. Her brows were arched to perfection, her makeup was professionally applied to accentuate high cheekbones, and her skin looked flawless. Yesterday, Evelyn Randolph's clothes hung off her petite frame, while today, a bright red dress clung to every curve of her body, and there were many.

"Va-va-voom," Nana Jo said over my shoulder.

Evelyn flashed a smile and gave a throaty laugh. "I decided to treat myself to a small makeover. Too much?"

"Heck no."

"You look amazing," I said.

"Thank you." She glanced around. "Where do you want me?"

I ushered her into my office, where I had a carton of books piled on a table with a chair and pen at the ready.

Evelyn Randolph sat down at the table and began signing.

I pulled out my cell phone. "Would you mind if I got a picture? We can use it for advertising."

"Certainly." She posed, and I snapped several pictures.

I wasn't sure how to start the conversation to find out if Evelyn killed Delia Marshall, or at the very least if she knew who might want her dead, when Evelyn opened the door.

"Terrible tragedy about Delia," she said casually. "It must have been a horrible shock for you."

"It was," I said.

She signed two more books. "How was it Delia happened to be here last night?"

I was confident the police wouldn't want the details known to the general public, but I needed Evelyn to talk and was going to have to give her something. "I have no idea. Something must have happened after she left yesterday. When you and Martha took her home, did she mention anything about coming back here?"

She shook her head. "No, she didn't say anything to us . . . but then Delia and I weren't that close."

Nana Jo sat on the sofa against the wall with Snickers in her lap and Oreo curled up next to her. "Really? I got the impression you all were longtime friends."

"No, we certainly weren't friends," she said too quickly. She must have realized how it came across because she added, "It is true that we've known each other a long time, but I wouldn't call us friends."

While Nana Jo and Evelyn talked, I studied the newly transformed author. Above the physical changes she'd made, there was something more. Evelyn Randolph wasn't just drop-dead gorgeous. She was confident, self-assured, and relaxed. I wondered why.

"Mrs. Randolph, you've known Delia Marshall for a long time, a lot longer than me," I said. "Do you know anyone who would have wanted to harm her? Anyone who might have wanted her dead?"

She finished signing her name before she turned to me. "Mrs. Washington, I—"

"Please call me Sam."

"And you can call me Evelyn." She smiled. "Sam, I'm going to be honest with you. Delia Marshall was a horrible human being. She was arrogant, nasty, vicious, and just plain ole mean."

"Why don't you tell us what you really think," Nana Jo mumbled.

"Sam, do you play chess?"

I shook my head.

"Well, you asked me if Delia Marshall and I were friends? We weren't. Delia didn't have friends. She had pawns. She had people in her life who she used to gain a tactical advantage."

I stared at Evelyn Randolph until she threw back her head and laughed.

"You're wondering what tactical advantage she got from me?" Evelyn asked.

I didn't need to look in a mirror to know that I was blushing. I could feel the heat rising up my neck.

Evelyn gazed out into space for a few seconds, then shook herself back to reality. "My only advantage to Delia was financial."

"I heard a rumor that she blackmailed people," I said.

"It's true. Delia really was smart. But rather than using her brains to help others, she used hers to sleuth out secrets. Everyone has secrets they'd rather weren't made public. Delia found out what they were and figured out how to use them to her benefit."

I took a deep breath. "Mrs. Randolph—"

"Evelyn."

"Evelyn, the police think I killed Delia. I have to figure out who did kill her. Anything you can tell me would be greatly appreciated."

"Anyone who spent more than fifteen minutes with her probably wanted to strangle her, including me." She smiled. "Sam, I like you. So, I'm going to tell you that Delia found out something about me . . . something I would have preferred to remain buried." She paused. "It's nothing sinister, but it is private."

"Was she blackmailing you?" Nana Jo asked.

"Yes. Delia found out that twenty-seven years ago, I entered this country illegally. My husband was . . . is a very wealthy, very cruel man. He heads a drug cartel in South America. When we met, I was just a teenager. I was flattered by the attention of this great man and the money he lavished on me. But he was evil. He threatened my family and me. When he started having affairs, I was actually excited. I thought maybe he'd get tired of me and let me leave." She shook her head. "I should have known better. It didn't matter if he wanted me or not. I was his property. Then, I made the biggest mistake ever . . . I got pregnant. There was no way he'd let me leave with my baby. So, I had to escape. I came to America. I changed my name. Learned English so well, no one can tell I have an accent."

"Except when you get angry," I said softly. "*Dios mío.*"

"You caught that? I thought so. I've lived in constant fear that someone would find out the truth and send me back. For years, I paid Delia to keep my secret. She made me pay practically every dime I had. I was miserable." She stared at me and leaned forward. "You inspired me. You came into that room like a . . . giant. You weren't afraid of Delia. You knew she could destroy your career, but you still burst into that room and challenged her. You weren't afraid of Delia Marshall. That's when I gained courage. I knew I needed to do something."

"What did you do?" I asked.

"I didn't kill her if that's what you're asking. I did make a decision. I decided to stop being a mouse and to stand up to her. I knew I had to face her. I was prepared to fight." She smiled. "But I didn't have to. Delia's dead, and my troubles are over. Well, most of them, anyway. I felt like I needed to do something to celebrate."

Evelyn Randolph didn't look like a woman who'd just killed someone, but that didn't mean she didn't.

"What about your baby?" Nana Jo asked.

"Maricela is married with a baby of her own. She was born here. She and her baby are safe."

"But you aren't?" I asked. "Surely they won't deport you after twenty-seven years."

"No. I'm an American citizen now. That's not my fear."

"Your husband?" Nana Jo asked.

She nodded. "But I heard that he is not well. Maybe he will die soon. Delia Marshall is dead. Perhaps soon, he will be, too."

I shivered. I liked Evelyn, and I felt sorry for her, but she certainly had a lot to gain from Delia Marshall's death.

Chapter 13

Evelyn signed the books and then hurried off. She had a date.

"That went a lot better than I thought," Nana Jo said once we were alone. "I didn't expect her to volunteer so much information. I wish everyone was that easy. Maybe we'll luck out and the killer will confess like they do on those old episodes of *Perry Mason*."

I smiled. "Sadly, real life doesn't work that way. In real life, people don't tell the truth. Even innocent people lie. They lie about things that are easy to figure out, too. I think it was in Rex Stout's *Three Doors to Death* when Nero Wolfe gives one of my favorite lines. Wolfe tells a suspect, '*Any fool could solve the most difficult of cases if everyone told the truth.*'"

Martha Chiswick arrived, but unlike Evelyn, she was all business. She sat at my desk and signed the same pile of books Evelyn Randolph had signed less than an hour earlier. I noticed that she made a point to sign her name above Evelyn's, even if it meant altering the size of the signature to do so. I've heard that order meant something to many people. I wondered if they'd negotiated that in their contract, that Martha's name would always appear first. She politely declined our

offer for coffee, tea, or snacks and focused on the task of signing her name.

Nana Jo and I both made a few attempts to get her to talk,
but on the rare instances when she responded with more than
a grunt, it was barely more than one or two words. She wasn't
rude, but she was also not going to indulge in a heart-to-heart
conversation.

I was tired. My lack of sleep was catching up with me. I
stifled a yawn and had to really work to stay focused and think
up something to say to her. "I'm terribly sorry to hear about
Delia's murder."

"Hmm."

"Do you know if she had any family?" Nana Jo asked.
"Perhaps we could call to give our condolences."

"Hmm. No idea."

I stifled a yawn. "I know it's early, but have you heard
anything about the funeral arrangements?"

"No. I haven't."

I glanced at Nana Jo, and she gave a slight shrug. Perhaps
the direct approach would be better. "Since she was murdered
here, the police have asked a ton of questions. Unfortunately,
I didn't know Delia very well. And, in the short time that I
did, she was . . . difficult. Do you, by any chance, know anyone who hated Delia enough to want to kill her?"

She paused signing her name for a brief moment, but it
didn't last long. She quickly resumed. "No."

If Martha Chiswick had secrets, she wasn't sharing them
with Nana Jo or me. Far too quickly, she'd signed all of the
books in the stack and was preparing to leave.

I needed to stall long enough to think up a way to engage
her in the conversation, but my brain wasn't cooperating.
Martha was gathering her things and rising to leave. My mind
went blank. In a panic, I blurted out, "Was Delia Marshall
blackmailing you?"

That got her attention.

All of the color drained from her face. She froze. Martha Chiswick looked like a ghost. She stared at me for a split second. She tore her gaze away. Her hand tremored, and she dropped her purse.

"Are you okay?" I asked.

"Perhaps you should sit down," Nana Jo said. "You look awful. Sam, get Martha a glass of water."

I headed toward the door but stopped when Martha said, "No, I'm fine."

She clearly wasn't fine, but I wasn't about to argue the point. "I'm sorry, I didn't mean to upset you. I just—"

"I know what you wanted," Martha said. "The police think you killed Delia, and you're trying to shift the blame. Well, you're not going to make me your patsy." She shook off Nana Jo's hand and rose. "It won't work. I didn't kill Delia."

"Mrs. Chiswick, I'm sorry. I—"

But Martha Chiswick wasn't listening. She reached down and picked up her purse from the floor. Clutching her purse to her chest, she hurried out the door.

Nana Jo and I stood staring at the door for a few seconds.

"Well, that went badly," Nana Jo said. "What were you trying to do, shock her into confessing?"

I yawned. "I don't know why I did that. I'm tired, and my brain isn't firing on all cylinders."

Nana Jo's face softened. "You look exhausted. Why don't you go upstairs and take a nap."

A nap sounded wonderful. "What are you going to do?"

"I'm meeting Freddie and his son for cocktails. If we're lucky, they'll have some information for us."

"I could use some luck," I said as I turned to head out of the room.

Detective Fieldstone took great pleasure in stating that my Market Street Mysteries was a crime scene and was going to be closed to the public. Jenna felt confident I'd be back up and running in a day. Two at the most. So, there wasn't much for me to do.

Once we were upstairs, I flopped down on the bed. Snickers jumped up after me and claimed her spot on the pillow. Oreo took his time, but eventually, he jumped up, and plopped down next to his big sister with his butt in her face, hiked his leg, and licked himself. After twelve years, Oreo had worn down Snickers's defenses to the point that she no longer growled, snapped, or bothered moving whenever he laid a paw on her. Instead, she sighed, stuck her muzzle under her paw, closed her eyes, and went to sleep. She was snoring before Oreo finished cleaning himself. We were all asleep shortly after our heads hit the pillow.

When I awoke, the room was dark, and Snickers's muzzle was inches from my face. Her eyes opened, and without thinking, I smiled. Snickers was fourteen, and I knew better than to open my mouth when she was close by. Without fail, she managed to stick her tongue in my mouth.

"Ugh." I rolled over and used my blanket to wipe my tongue and the inside of my mouth.

Snickers did a stretch I'd seen in my yoga class. The instructor called it Warrior III. At the first movement, Oreo was up and bouncing around on the bed like the Energizer Bunny.

I glanced at the clock and realized I'd only been asleep for three hours. It felt like I'd slept all night. I felt better. "I guess this is what they call a power nap," I said to Snickers.

She yawned.

"Come on. Let's go potty outside."

Snickers stretched again, but when I left the bedroom, she and Oreo followed.

When I passed through the living room, Nana Jo's head popped up from the sofa. "Good, you're up."

I jumped and clutched my heart. "You scared me."

"Sorry. I was reading." She held up a book. "I must have dozed off."

"Must not be a very exciting book." I glanced at the cover.

"It's Martha Chiswick and Evelyn Randolph's new book."

"Let me take the dogs outside, and you can tell me what you think when I get back."

"Let me take them. You better freshen up. We're supposed to meet everyone at Frank's in thirty minutes, and your hair looks like Don King's." Nana Jo stood up and headed for the stairs. "Come on."

Snickers and Oreo trotted after her, and I went to the bathroom. One glance in the mirror, and I chuckled. Nana Jo was right. My hair was standing straight up on one side and looked like a hot mess.

With only thirty minutes, I didn't have a ton of time, but I was in desperate need of a hot shower. I stripped off my clothes and hopped in. The steam refreshed me. I would have loved to have lingered, but I didn't have time. Instead, I dried off and pulled on a pair of clean jeans and a royal blue sweater that I knew Frank liked. I didn't have time to focus on my hair and my makeup. So, I beat my hair into submission and pulled it back into a ponytail, and then I took a few extra minutes to apply my makeup.

When I came out to the living room, Nana Jo hadn't changed clothes, but her lipstick looked fresh, and she was sitting on the sofa waiting.

"Sorry, I just really needed a shower."

Nana Jo waved her hand. "Understandable."

I took four dog biscuits out of the biscuit jar, and like the Pied Piper, the poodles followed me back to the bedroom. I dropped the biscuits where I knew each dog would get two. I asked *She Who Must Not Be Named* to play light jazz, then I turned out the lights and closed the door.

Nana Jo and I headed downstairs. On the way, she told me her thoughts about Martha and Evelyn's book.

"It was interesting. It's a story about two women, Maryanne and Carol. They met in college. Carol was really shy, but she met a young man, Chuck, and fell head over heels. But Chuck was more interested in Maryanne. One day, Carol and Maryanne get into a huge fight. When Chuck tries to break it up, they accidentally knock him over the head. He falls down, hits his head, and dies. The girls are shocked and scared, and rather than going to the police and confessing everything, they cover it up. They toss Chuck's body into Lake Michigan. Somehow, Carol convinces Maryanne that it's all her fault and she's solely responsible for Chuck's death."

"Hmm. Let me guess. Carol blackmails Maryanne?"

"You got it. She waits ten years until Maryanne is married to a highly successful judge. Then, she blackmails her." Nana Jo opened the door to the North Harbor Café and held it for me to enter.

"Fiction imitating life?" I asked.

"Guess what Martha Chiswick's husband does?"

"Judge?"

She nodded. "You got it."

We walked around the crowds and headed upstairs. The same crowd from earlier today was present with one addition. Ruby Mae had invited her godson, Dr. Geoffrey Allen, to join us.

Nana Jo and I took our seats.

Frank was a wine connoisseur who hoped that I would join in his appreciation. So far, he hadn't found the right wine for me, but that didn't stop him from trying. He handed me a glass with a light pink wine.

I sniffed it as he'd instructed and took a sip.

He anxiously watched my face. "Well?"

I shrugged. "It's okay. What is it?"

"An award-winning Moscato."

"I don't know why you keep wasting your time," Jenna said. "You'd be better off picking up a five-dollar bottle of Ripple from the gas station. I, on the other hand, love Moscato."

I passed the glass across the table.

She took a sip, closed her eyes, and sighed. "That's delicious. Do I taste apples?"

She and Frank talked about hints, aromas, bouquets, and grapes while my attention wandered. Frank forever sealed his place in my sister's heart when he promised to give her a bottle. Nana Jo pulled out her iPad, and all discussion ended.

"We don't have a lot of time," Jenna said, "although I have it on good authority that the district attorney will be making doubly sure that his case is rock solid before issuing a warrant for Sam's arrest."

Everyone looked at Jenna. She'd agreed not to disclose Frank's role in the matter, but the lie didn't sit well. She hid her face by taking a sip of wine, but I saw the color rise up her neck.

"Okay, who wants to go first?" Nana Jo asked.

"I invited my godson, Geoff, to join the meeting today, I hope that's okay?" Ruby Mae looked around the table, and seeing no objections, she turned to Geoff. "Go ahead and tell them what you told me."

"When my book was released, Delia Marshall tried to extort money from me," Allen said.

When the murmur died down, Jenna asked the question we all wanted to know.

"How?"

"She told me that if I wanted a good review, I'd have to pay her five thousand dollars." Allen shook his head. "Which was crazy. I'm an academic. There's no way my book would net that kind of money."

"What do you mean?" I asked.

"I'm a professor of criminal psychology. My book isn't sexy. It's not going to be on the *New York Times* Best Seller list. It's only going to appeal to an incredibly small market— mostly other academics."

"But you interviewed the pope and won a BAFTA. Surely, that would provide publicity that would—"

He was shaking his head before I finished talking. "The interview with the pope was amazing, but that was for a documentary. Sadly, winning awards doesn't always translate into money."

"Then why do it?" Irma asked.

"I love my work." He leaned forward, and his eyes sparkled as he talked. "I find it fascinating digging into why someone kills. What's going on inside their head that compels someone to take a life."

"So, you do it for the thrill?" Dorothy asked.

"I guess so . . . at least partly." He chuckled and leaned back. "Don't get me wrong. Apart from the internal gratification I get from the study, as an academic, I'm expected to publish a scholarly work. I guess there's the pride and recognition of my peers and the prestige that it brings to the university."

"Bulls—"

"Irma!" we all shouted.

Irma broke into a coughing fit. She knocked back the whiskey she'd ordered earlier and held up her glass to get another. "Sorry, but Sam has been slaving over her books for years. I don't believe anyone would put in that kind of work and not get any money."

"I got an advance from my publisher, but most of that money was used to pay my research assistant. Plus, there's the editing, and . . . like I said, academic publishing is different."

"I'm with Mrs. Starczewski down there," Detective Pitt

said. He took a sip of beer and used his sleeve to wipe the foam from his mouth. "You mean to tell me, Delia Marshall tries to extort money from you in exchange for a good review, and you do nothing? Extortion is illegal. How come you didn't report her to the police?"

"That's the problem. Delia never came right out and asked for money."

"What did she do?" Jenna asked.

Allen thought for several moments. "She talked about the power of positive reviews and how it could launch careers. Then she bemoaned the fact that reviewers didn't get paid, even though they often did more to launch a book than literary agents who got paid fifteen percent of their royalties or even a publicist who got a lot more than that."

"But these are legitimate businesses, not undercover deals," I said.

"I wonder what would have happened if the newspapers who syndicated her column found out what she was doing?" Nana Jo said.

"I thought of that, but Delia was smart," Allen said. "She never asked for money directly in exchange for a good review. She also mentioned that her role was simply a go-between. She had an offshore account, and the money was to be transferred in."

"That aligns with what I found out about her bank accounts," Frank said. After getting a nod from Dr. Allen to continue, he said, "I found out that Delia Marshall had offshore bank accounts in Singapore, Switzerland, and the Cayman Islands."

"Why so many?" I asked.

"Probably for security. If anything happens in Singapore, then she has money in the others. At least, that's my source's best guess."

"How much money are you talking about?" Nana Jo asked.

"So far, he's guessing she's squirreled away two-point-four million."

"Dollars?" I asked.

"Yeah, he's still searching, and there may be more, but she set up several pass-through companies, and it's taking a bit of time, but he should have it worked out by tomorrow." Frank squeezed my hand under the table.

I mouthed, *Thank you,* and squeezed back.

"Delia Marshall was definitely smart," Allen said. "She made sure she never said anything that could *prove* what she was up to. It was hard to prove what she was doing, and . . . while I wasn't going to pay her, I also didn't want to get involved in a long police investigation that could have led to a lawsuit and legal fees. I guess I should have reported it, but . . ."

Detective Pitt scowled. "You should have. How do you expect the police to do their job and get criminals off the street if citizens don't report these things?"

I took a sip of water and avoided making eye contact, but Jenna was braver than me.

"In a perfect world, I'd agree with you, but we don't live in perfect, and Dr. Allen is correct."

Detective Pitt started to interject, but Jenna held up a hand to stop him.

"As an officer of the court, I agree with you. However, I've seen how unscrupulous people like Delia Marshall play on the flaws within the system and use them to their advantage. They tie up the wheels of justice until careers are ruined. Does anyone mind if I go next?" She glanced around. Seeing no objections, she continued. "I had a talk with the district attorney. He was familiar with Delia Marshall, by the way. He told me about one of his attorneys who had a run-in with her."

Jenna took a sip of her wine. "Preston Kincaid used to work for the district attorney. He was smart, hardworking, well liked, and ambitious. He had political aspirations, and everyone thought he was on the fast track to the capital and the governor's office. That was until Delia accused him of misconduct."

"Any truth to the allegations?" Dorothy Clark asked. "They always say there's no smoke without fire."

"Apparently, her allegations were false, so Kincaid chose to fight rather than settling out of court."

Detective Pitt shot a smug look in Dr. Allen's direction. "Good for him."

"Not really," Jenna said. "Delia raked up so much muck that Preston's career was ruined. No more talks about moving to Lansing. No more dreams about a life in politics. Preston claimed he was over it, but I think he's still bitter."

"Who wouldn't be?" I said. "I don't suppose Preston Kincaid has an alibi for the time of the murder?"

"What time was she killed?" Nana Jo asked.

All eyes turned to Detective Pitt.

Pitt pulled a small notepad from his pocket. He flipped a few pages until he found what he was looking for. "I'm still technically on medical leave, so it wasn't as easy to get information as it normally is. According to what I could find out from the coroner, which wasn't much"—he mumbled a few words that implied he questioned Detective Fieldstone's parentage before he continued—"Delia Marshall was murdered sometime between twelve o'clock when she called you"—he glanced in my direction—"and two o'clock when you discovered her body in the bookstore. Cause of death was blunt force trauma."

Dorothy Clark raised her hand. "If you're done, I'd like to go next."

Detective Pitt nodded.

"I don't really have much to tell, not yet anyway. I went to the book reading, and Jillian was right. He's looking for investors and has latched onto me."

"I wondered why you were wearing the crown jewels tonight," Nana Jo said. "You're going to need a security guard to make sure you don't get bashed on the head like Delia."

Detective Pitt's eyes grew large. "Wait, you mean all that's real?"

"Of course it's real," Dorothy said.

"It's a wonder you can lift your hand under all those rocks," Nana Jo said.

Frank whistled. "Nana Jo's right. You might need a bodyguard with all that ice."

"My late husband gave me these." Dorothy smiled. "Delia Marshall kept her money in banks outside the country, but it took over seventy years for my husband's family to get back the money their relatives had deposited into Swiss banks during the second world war when they fled Germany."

"That's horrible," I said.

"Back in 1995, the World Jewish Congress, or WJC, sued the Swiss banks to recover the money. It took five years, but the WJC won a 1.25 billion dollar settlement. Nothing is one hundred percent safe, but jewels can be worn or sewn into clothing and hidden." Dorothy glanced at her jewels and sighed. "Anyway, I pulled all of this out and strutted around the reading like I was the queen of England. Denver Benedict fawned all over me. We're going to dinner tonight. I hope to have something to report by tomorrow morning."

I shared what we'd learned from Evelyn Randolph and promised to tackle Martha Chiswick again, now that I was rested.

"Well, the only thing I found out was that Martha Chiswick and Evelyn Randolph were researching another book," Nana Jo said.

"Maybe they're working on a sequel to their first book," Dorothy said. "That's hardly newsworthy. You're hiding something."

Nana Jo smiled. "My source insisted the women weren't working on a sequel. My source says they were furious about how Delia trashed their first book and wanted revenge. This new book was an exposé about their good friend Delia Marshall."

"Really?" I said. "I can't imagine Delia would have been too thrilled if she'd found out about that."

Nana Jo nodded. "My thoughts exactly. Next time we talk to Martha, we need to find out if Delia knew what they were up to."

We talked for a few minutes, but Irma and Dorothy both had dinner dates and had to leave.

Dr. Allen came around the table and whispered that he had a meeting and needed to go.

"I'd be glad to drive Ruby Mae home," I offered.

"She said you'd probably take her." He smiled and then became serious. "You didn't ask, but for what it's worth, I wanted you to know that I have an alibi."

I started to object, but he held up his hand to stop me.

"It's okay. I know you need to figure out who murdered her. And to be fair, you need to consider everyone as a suspect. No matter who they're related to." He grinned. "For the record, Ruby Mae and about fifty of my relatives were having a get-together. It started at eight, and I didn't get in bed until after two. I was surrounded by family, who will all verify that I never left." He patted my arm. "I wanted you to know."

"Thank you, but I never considered you a suspect."

Jenna, Nana Jo, Ruby Mae, Detective Pitt, and I ordered dinner. Frank was called down to the kitchen.

The food was fantastic. Nana Jo managed to get my mind

off Delia Marshall when she asked how I was progressing with the wedding plans.

Frank and I had decided to get married in just three months. With everything going on, including the possibility that I could be spending the next fifteen to twenty years in jail, I hadn't had time to think about it. Or worry about meeting Frank's mother and the rest of his family and undercover spy friends. Honestly, I wasn't sure which was worse, thinking about going to prison or planning a wedding. My late husband, Leon, and I solved this by eloping. I think if I did that again, my mother would strangle me.

"We're going to have a small wedding with only family and close friends," I said.

"I know that's what you want, but is that what Frank wants?" Ruby Mae asked.

"Good point," Jenna said. "This is his first marriage, isn't it?"

"Yes, it's his first marriage," I said. "And, yes, this is what Frank wants."

"What is?" Frank slipped up the stairs and sat down.

"A small wedding," I said.

"I want whatever will make Sam happy." He took my hand and kissed it.

Wait, what does that mean? I thought he wanted a small wedding. Is he only agreeing to a small wedding because he knows that's what I want? I don't want to cheat him out of a big wedding if that's what he really wants.

Frank read my mind, leaned close, and whispered, "Stop stressing. I would prefer a small wedding. Actually, I'm fine with going to the justice of the peace tonight." He grinned.

"Are you sure? What about your mom? She won't be disappointed, will she?"

"I have no idea, but it's not her wedding, so I really don't care. Honestly, I think she'll be happy to know that I'm happily married to the love of my life."

He kissed me, and for a few minutes, all thoughts of weddings, murder, and everything else vanished.

"I'm sorry to interrupt, but we have another problem in the kitchen," Morgan, our server, said.

"Remind me to fire her," Frank mumbled as he rose from his seat and followed her downstairs.

We wrapped up and went our separate ways, with plans to meet back at Market Street Mysteries tomorrow.

Nana Jo and I walked back to the bookshop. She went to her room to finish reading Martha and Evelyn's book, and I went to my room.

The problem with naps is that when it's bedtime, I'm rarely tired. I still had a few hours before I needed to go to sleep, so maybe a little writing would help me make sense of the things that I'd learned tonight.

Lady Elizabeth, Lord James Browning, and Thompkins found themselves back in the king's drawing room, but this time, the king had conveniently not joined. Lady Elizabeth and Lord Browning were joined by their spouses, Lord William Marsh and Lady Daphne. The group also included Lord Victor and Lady Penelope Carlston, Lady Clara, and Detective Peter Covington.

Once everyone was seated, Lady Elizabeth didn't hesitate. "There's been a murder, and His Royal Highness, King George, has asked for our help in solving it."

Detective Covington hopped up. "A murder? Has Scotland Yard been called in?"

Lady Clara clasped the detective's hand. "Darling,

perhaps you should allow Aunt Elizabeth to finish so she can tell us."

"Sorry, please continue." The detective returned to his seat.

"The local constables are aware of the situation, as are a few divisions within . . . other branches of the government," Lady Elizabeth said. "Due to the precarious nature of things at the moment, it was determined that the fewer people who are aware of this, the better."

She shared everything they'd learned from the king about the situation to the group and then turned to Lord Browning and Thompkins. "Did I miss anything?"

They both shook their heads.

"Peter, I'm hoping you can get us information from the coroner," Lady Elizabeth said to the detective. "Hopefully, the time of death and well . . . anything else they can provide."

Detective Covington nodded.

Lady Elizabeth pulled out her knitting. She checked her stitches and then turned to her husband. "Milicent Schmidt was a reporter with the *London Times*. Isn't the editor, Geoffrey Fordham-Baker, a member of your club?"

"He is. Fourth son of the Second Viscount of Lampton. I'll pop over to the club and see if I can find the fellow. I'll stand him a few glasses of port." The duke chuckled. "That should loosen his lips."

"Good, but be careful, dear. If I remember, Geoffrey is a bottomless pit where port is concerned. I don't want your gout flaring up again."

"Bloody awful thing, gout. Sucks the joy out of life." Lord William puffed on his pipe and grumbled.

Lady Elizabeth stopped to concentrate on her knitting. After a brief moment, she continued. "James, do you think you could find out if there was anything in the papers found from the red box that might have been a motive for her murder?"

Lord Browning smiled. "I've already contacted my sources at Downing Street, and I'm going to meet with the king's private secretary, Clive Elliott, as soon as we're finished here. I should have something by this afternoon."

"Wonderful." Lady Elizabeth smiled at her nephew. "It's so useful to have someone with your . . . connections at a time like this." She finished a complicated stitch and then turned to her niece. "Daphne, Cousin Lucille is here. Have you seen her?"

Lady Daphne scowled. "I've tried not to."

"Well, she is Elizabeth's lady-in-waiting."

"Lucille Redding is also the biggest gossip." Daphne sighed. "Oh, all right. If there's any gossip to be had, she'll know what it is. I'll stop hiding and invite myself to tea."

"Thank you, dear. It's all for a worthy cause." Lady Elizabeth knitted. "Now, Clara, aren't you friends with that young woman who writes for the *Daily Telegraph*?"

"Claire Hollingworth. She's brilliant."

"I'm hoping that journalists are a tight-knit group. There can't be a lot of women journalists, not yet anyway. I was hoping you could see if she knew Milicent."

"Certainly, but . . ." Lady Clara stood up and paced in front of the fireplace. "Something's bothering me about that piece of lace you showed us."

"I know. It's bothering me, too. There's something wrong there, but I haven't figured out what it is yet. I was hoping Penelope might be able to help us with that one."

"Me? I don't knit or crochet or whatever that is." She pointed at the scrap that Lady Elizabeth placed on the coffee table.

"True, but the shawl was a gift. It was given to the queen mother by her goddaughter, Alice."

"Alice Jamison?" Lady Penelope asked.

Lady Elizabeth nodded. "She went to Manor House School in Limpsfield with your cousin Mary Churchill. She gave the shawl to the queen mother." Lady Elizabeth glanced at the scrap of lace and frowned. "There's something . . . unusual, and I can't put my finger on it. Maybe Alice can tell you where she got it."

Lord Browning stepped forward. "I did find out one piece of information from one of the royal guardsmen. Schmidt was overheard arguing with a Lieutenant Jamison the day she was murdered."

"Jamison?" Victor asked. "Would that be Lieutenant Roland Jamison?"

Lord Browning nodded.

"I went to school with Roland. Fine chap. I can have a talk with him, unless . . ." He glanced around.

"That would be perfect," Lady Elizabeth said, smiling. Then she turned to the butler. "Thompkins, we'll need you to see what the servants know."

The butler gave a curt nod.

"I think that's everyone." Lady Elizabeth intercepted frightened looks between her nieces and young cousin. "What's bothering you ladies? Surely, you're not worried that we can't figure out who murdered that poor woman?"

"To be completely honest, I'm more worried about what happens if we do," Lady Penelope said.

"Bertie may be king, but he's always been fair," Lady Elizabeth said. "I don't believe he'd murder anyone. If he did, he'd hardly be likely to ask us here to find out who did. No, I'm sure the king isn't involved." She gazed into the fireplace for several moments.

"And who are you going to tackle?" Lady Clara asked.

"I'm going to put my head in the lion's mouth." Lady Elizabeth sighed. "I'm going to interview the queen mother."

"May God help your soul," Lady Clara whispered.

Chapter 14

"Sam, wake up."

"What's wrong? Is it another tornado?" I leaped up from the desk where I'd fallen asleep.

"No, but you need to get showered," Nana Jo said. "Everyone will be here in about thirty minutes. The girls have the information they want to share, so I moved our meeting time up. Frank's bringing a continental breakfast. I don't think you're ready for your betrothed to see you like that, are you?"

I glanced at my face in the dresser mirror and gasped. "How much time do I have?"

Nana Jo glanced at her watch. "Less than thirty minutes. You get showered and beat your hair into submission, and I'll take the poodles outside and get the conference room ready."

It took me a bit longer than thirty minutes, but not much. I gave up on controlling my hair, shoved my unruly mane into a hat, and focused on makeup. By the time I came downstairs, everyone was enjoying the pastries, fruit, and coffee Frank had brought.

I grabbed a cup of coffee and slid into a seat next to Frank. "Thank you," I whispered.

"You know I love to cook, and I especially love watching people eat. So, it was my pleasure. Besides, I'm considering accepting more catering jobs and this gives me an opportunity to practice."

Nana Jo normally waited until everyone was done eating before starting meetings, but she pulled out her iPad early today. "Several people have to leave early, so we're going to start and let them get about their day."

Frank cleared his throat. "I'm one of those people who has to get to work, so if it's okay, I'd like to go first."

No one objected.

"My source was able to get a bit more information on Delia Marshall's offshore accounts." He pulled a paper out of his pocket, and I looked over his shoulder at the names. "He was able to trace a few of the deposits."

"Martha Chiswick, Evelyn Randolph, and Denver Benedict were all paying large sums of money to Delia Marshall," I said.

"How could he trace them so quickly?" Nana Jo asked.

"I gave him some names of the people involved that we know about. He could correlate the dates that large sums were withdrawn from one account and match it to large sums deposited to Delia Marshall. Plus, he's got other ways that I can't talk about, but trust me. He's good at what he does."

"We aren't questioning your source," Nana Jo said.

"Evelyn told us that she'd been paying Delia, but she denied killing her," I said.

"All killers lie," Detective Pitt added.

"We'll need to find another way to get Martha Chiswick to talk," Nana Jo said.

"That's all I've got, and I need to get back down to the restaurant." Frank stood and glanced at me. "If we're still on for dinner, you can fill me in tonight and give me any new assignments."

I nodded. "Thank you."

"Thanks for breakfast," everyone said.

"I've got to leave for work, too," Jenna said. "I'm looking into some of the lawsuits Delia Marshall filed. Someone might have resented her enough to kill her. I should have more information tonight." She got up and left.

"I guess I'm next," Detective Pitt said. "I've been assigned light desk duty, so I'm back on the force."

"Congratulations," everyone said.

"I should be able to get a look at the full police file." Detective Pitt grabbed two pastries and walked out.

Dorothy Clark raised her hand. "I can confirm that Delia Marshall was definitely blackmailing Denver Benedict."

"He admitted it?" I asked.

Dorothy nodded.

"What did she have on him?" Nana Jo asked.

"Apparently, Delia found out that the articles he wrote about the five years he supposedly spent in a North Korean prison were all fake news."

Questions flew faster than Dorothy could supply answers. *What? That's incredible! How could he get away with something like that?*

Nana Jo held up her hand to stop the tirade. "Hold your horses. Give the woman a chance to breathe."

Dorothy smiled her thanks at Nana Jo and took a sip of water and a deep breath. "Apparently, he was bumming his way across Asia and feeling depressed about his journalism career. That's when he spent a night drinking too much soju and got the idea to fake the story."

"But he won a Pulitzer and practically every other award a journalist can win," Nana Jo said. "Didn't anyone check the story out to make sure it was true?"

"Apparently not. I gathered that the authorities in that region of the world weren't very forthcoming with information.

He was pretty much in the middle of nowhere, so no one could confirm his stories, nor could they debunk them."

"Then how'd Delia Marshall figure it out?" Nana Jo asked.

Dorothy shrugged. "No idea. She might have just been shooting in the dark, but regardless, she got a hit. He swears he has no idea how Delia found out the truth, but she's bilked him for every dime he has."

"Why'd he pay her?" I asked.

"He said his reputation would have suffered, and his career would be over." Dorothy shrugged. "I almost felt sorry for him, but . . ."

"I feel so disillusioned," I said. "I loved his writing." I'd read Benedict's account of his time in that North Korean prison practically every year from the time I was twelve until I was thirty. He was a brilliant writer. His words painted a vibrant picture of horror. I cried at the pain and suffering he'd described. Now I felt betrayed. How many other people felt the same? I begrudgingly acknowledged that he was a brilliant writer, if a dishonest one. He'd claimed the story was true. Would he be stripped of his awards? Could he be sued? If word got out, publishers might not want to publish more of his books. Maybe I could discreetly ask my editor what the ramifications would be for something like this. I felt confident that Denver Benedict's reputation would be forever tainted. But would that be enough to drive him to murder?

"Did Denver Benedict have an alibi for Sunday night when Delia was murdered?" I asked.

"He claimed he was home in bed . . . alone." Dorothy narrowed her gaze. "I'm not sure I believe him."

"Which part?" Nana Jo asked.

"The alone part." She shook her head. "He was so busy trying to charm me into investing, I get the feeling that Denver Benedict doesn't spend very many nights alone."

"Do you think you can get him to tell you the truth?" I asked.

"I'll get the truth out of him if I have to use brute force," Dorothy said. "I'm having dinner with him tonight. Don't you worry, Sam."

"Please be careful. He could be a murderer," I reminded her.

"I'm always careful."

Ruby Mae looked up from her knitting. "Well, I didn't get anything else."

Irma patted her hair. "I had a wonderful time with Bernie last night."

Nana Jo rolled her eyes. "Did you learn anything useful?"

"Well, I don't know if I learned anything new, but I taught Bernie a couple of things." She smiled.

"IRMA!" Nana Jo yelled.

"Oh, you mean about the murder. Well, Bernie said Delia Marshall was very tight-lipped. She didn't try to blackmail him. In fact, I got the distinct impression that Delia tried to flirt with him. Can you imagine that?" Irma glanced around with a shocked look.

"Imagine that," Nana Jo said sarcastically.

"Bernie also owns the maintenance company that handled the repairs and lawn work. Anyway, he said Delia was always calling him to come to fix something that didn't need fixing. He lived nearby and used to get her mail when she was out of town, and he just happened to have a spare key to her post office box." Irma reached down the front of her blouse and pulled out a key on a plastic key ring. She held it up and dangled it in the air. "He let me borrow it."

I stared at the key in stunned silence.

"What's in there?" Nana Jo asked.

"He didn't know. He hasn't opened it." Irma flashed a smile.

"Well, there's only one way to find out." Nana Jo snapped her iPad closed and stood.

Everyone stood but me. I was still staring at that key like I was hypnotized.

Nana Jo waved her hand in front of my face. "Earth to Sam."

"There might be evidence in that box," I said.

"I hope so. That's why we're going." Nana Jo held the back of her hand against my forehead as though she were taking my temperature. "Are you feeling okay?"

"But that's evidence, isn't it? I mean, we need to take that to the police." I glanced around. "I wish Stinky Pitt was still here." I flinched. I'd made a conscientious effort to avoid using that childhood nickname, and here it slipped out. "I mean, Detective Pitt."

Nana Jo turned to Irma. "Did Bernie say if he'd been questioned by the police?"

"Detective Fieldstone questioned him. He said he told them he often picked up Delia's mail when she was out of town." She paused. "I don't know if he told them about the spare key or not."

"Maybe they got a court order or something and opened it already," I said. "It could be empty."

"Or Detective Fieldstone may not think there is any evidence in that post office box that would incriminate you, the only suspect he's interested in, so he didn't follow through," Nana Jo said. "In which case, we could get lucky."

Irma smiled. "I sure got lucky last night. Bernie has a really big—"

"IRMA!"

Irma broke into a coughing fit. When she was able to talk, she said, "I was going to say, apartment." She grinned in a way that told all of us that she was lying.

Nana Jo grabbed me by the shoulders and pulled me to my feet. "If it makes you feel better, you can call Jenna and ask her, but you and I both know that Fieldstone and Deevers think you killed Delia Marshall. They aren't interested in finding out who killed her. Now, we need to get moving."

In a daze, I allowed myself to be ushered out to my car. I don't remember driving to the post office, but I must have because I parked right next to the building.

Everyone got out while I sat behind the wheel.

Nana Jo came to the driver's window and opened the door. "Come along, Sam. All for one and one for all."

I got out of the car and followed my grandmother and the others into the building.

North Harbor wasn't large enough to have more than one post office, and that one was small and serviced both North and South Harbor. The post office was a small redbrick building located just a few blocks from the police station and courthouse, which would be convenient if I got arrested for tampering with the United States mail.

Inside, the building was surprisingly crowded. I had a notion that technology had made places like the post office a thing of the past. Did anyone send letters anymore? I, like practically everyone else I knew, paid bills online. I sent e-mails and text messages and couldn't remember the last time I'd written a letter by hand. Based on the number of people in this small building, the post office had not gone the way of the dodo bird. Glancing around, it appeared the post office had reinvented itself into more of a retail establishment, selling not just stamps but envelopes, boxes, and packaging supplies. Social distancing contributed to the congestion, as people stood on stickers stuck to the ground that measured six feet apart. Once in the front door, there was another door to the left that led into the main retail area of the building. The retail store was limited to no more than four customers, so the line extended out into the lobby.

To the right of the lobby was an alcove of post office boxes of varying sizes. The key had the number of the box. Delia Marshall had one of the larger post office boxes.

"Nana Jo, I don't know if we should do this." I glanced around to make sure no strangers could overhear our conversation.

"Don't be silly." Nana Jo stuck the key into the lock.

I reached out to stop her. "Tampering with the US mail is a federal crime. I think we should take that key to the police station. I'm in enough trouble as it is."

"You aren't tampering with the mail. We were *given* the key. We're simply following up on a lead. If we find that this box contains bills and supermarket flyers, we can leave it for the police. But, if we find something that could lead us to Delia Marshall's killer, then . . . we can consider handing it over to the police." Nana Jo twisted the key in the lock and mumbled, "*After* we solve the case."

Nana Jo opened the box and reached inside. She pulled out a packet of mail held together with a large rubber band and flipped through it. The bulk of the box contained bills, supermarket flyers, and pizza and oil change coupons. One of the last items was a pocket-sized journal. Nana Jo held up the journal. "Bingo!"

Chapter 15

"What is that?" I asked.

"I don't know. Let's get out of here and find out." Nana Jo stuffed everything else back into the box, turned the key, and marched out of the post office.

I hesitated a moment but quickly followed her and the girls outside.

In the safety of the car, Nana Jo flipped open the journal while the rest of us looked on silently.

"What is it, Josephine?" Dorothy asked from the back seat.

"It's some kind of journal." Nana Jo frowned as she scanned the pages.

"What does it say?" Ruby Mae asked.

"I have no idea. It's all in some kind of code."

That peeked my interest. I leaned across the front seat and glanced at the journal. "Code? What kind of code?"

Each page of the journal contained a series of numbers separated by dashes.

"That's suspicious," Ruby Mae said from the back seat.

"It sure is," Nana Jo said. "This may be just what we need to crack the case."

I flung questions like a pitcher at a fast-pitch softball game. "But why was it in her post office box? How did it get there? Did she mail it to herself?"

"If I knew that, then I'd have solved the case."

"Wait." I took a deep breath. "This is evidence. We need to get this to the police."

"How do we know it's evidence?" Dorothy said. "We don't even know what it is."

"That's right," Nana Jo said. "Maybe this is the way Delia Marshall kept track of her Weight Watchers points."

"Weight Watchers?" I stared at my grandmother. "How do you know Delia Marshall used Weight Watchers?"

She shrugged. "I don't know that she did, but you don't know that she didn't."

"Why don't you ask Jenna?" Ruby Mae said.

"Good idea," I said. I pushed the "talk" button and told the car to call my sister.

Jenna picked up. "What?"

"FYI, I'm in the car with Nana Jo and the girls, and you're on speaker." I liked to warn people whenever conversations weren't private. "Anyway, Irma got a key for Delia Marshall's post office box and—"

"WHAT?"

I was so confident that my sister would confirm that I was right that I failed to prepare myself appropriately for the pit bull response. "We got a key—"

"Please tell me you didn't use the key?"

Unlike my sister, when I was upset, my voice was quieter. My sister's voice boomed through the car, and I pressed the "volume down" button several times.

After a long pause, Jenna said, "Well?"

"You said to tell you we didn't use the key. Since we did, I didn't—"

"Stop. Stop talking. Sam, do you mean to tell me that you took that key and opened Delia Marshall's post office box?"

I glanced at my grandmother. "Uh-huh."

"Are you crazy?" Jenna said a bit more, but it was easier to let her get the rant off her chest and not interrupt.

So, we sat quietly while my sister questioned my sanity. We were all silent, but Nana Jo wasn't idle. She pulled out her cell phone and started taking pictures of the pages in the journal.

"Sam?" Jenna yelled. "Are you listening?"

"Yep. I just want to say that I tried to convince Nana Jo this wasn't a good idea. I—"

"Stop talking."

I didn't need to watch my sister to know that she was rubbing the side of her head.

"Take that journal to the police station at once. Ask for Detective Deevers. I'll meet you there."

"Jenna, we . . . hello . . . hello?" I ended the call. "She hung up."

"Boy, she can go from zero to sixty in no time flat," Dorothy said.

"I used to date a guy who could—"

"IRMA!"

I put the car in gear and backed out of my parking space.

"Where do you think you're going?" Nana Jo asked.

"The police station. You heard Jenna."

"Yeah, I heard her, but you don't have to hurry." Nana Jo continued snapping pictures.

The post office was less than two blocks away from the police station, so the trip didn't take long, no matter how slowly I drove. I pulled into the parking lot.

Before getting out of the car, I turned to Nana Jo. "Don't

forget to leave your Peacemaker in the glove box. I don't want a repeat of that experience."

Nana Jo opened her purse and put the gun she almost always carried with her in the glove compartment. "You're never going to let me forget that, are you?"

"Considering we were pushed to the ground with a squadron of police pointing guns at us . . . no. I'm not." I got out of the car and slammed the door.

The North Harbor courthouse and police station were combined into one building to decrease the costs. Both shared the parking lot and the strategically positioned metal detectors.

Nana Jo, the girls, and I walked in and put our belongings on the conveyor belt and then walked through the metal detectors. I went first. No bells or alarms went off, but I couldn't exhale until the last person cleared the contraption without incident. I think the police must have a picture of Nana Jo hidden somewhere with a title like *Caution if you see this woman!* because two of the policemen watched her like hawks, but they must have also been warned because while they stared, they didn't engage her.

We grabbed our belongings and walked to the left toward the lobby of the police station.

The courage I'd felt earlier evaporated by the time I got to the counter, and I stared at that officer for a few moments. I couldn't remember why I was there or who I wanted to see for the life of me. I stammered, "Can we . . . s-s-see. I mean, we're here to t-t-talk . . . well, we don't really want to t-t-talk. Actually, it's more like we have s-s-some information, but it's not really information. It's more like—"

Nana Jo poked me in the back. The poke helped force the words out of my head.

"Can we see Stinky Pitt . . . I mean, Detective Bradley Pitt."

The desk sergeant pointed to the hard folding chairs in the waiting room and pointed for us to sit down.

I sat and rested my head against the wall.

Nana Jo whispered, "What's wrong with you? You've been to the police station before, and you've solved a boatload of murders. I've never seen you completely fall apart."

"I don't know. I think it's being here and knowing that, unlike Detective Pitt, Detectives Fieldstone and Deevers actually believe I did it. They have a lot of circumstantial evidence, and they *want* to arrest me."

Nana Jo put her arm around my shoulders and gave me a squeeze. "We're not going to let that happen. Between your sister the pit bull, and your fiancé, who's some kind of a cross between James Bond and the Equalizer, we'll get you out of this one way or another."

I stared at my grandmother. "The Equalizer?"

"You know, Robert McCall . . . the Equalizer. It was a television show back in the eighties with that British actor with the sexy accent, and then Denzel Washington did a remake. Boy, was he hot."

Irma sat up and glanced around. "Who? Where?"

"Down, girl." Nana Jo shook her head. "We're just talking."

I grinned. "I know who the Equalizer is. I just never thought of Frank like that."

"Well, he's got all of these high-level, secret connections, speaks a million languages, and . . . there's just something about him that screams a if-you-mess-with-me-I'll-kill-you-with-a-gum-wrapper-and-no-one-will-ever-touch-me vibe." She stared at me. "It's pretty darned sexy, too. You're a lucky woman."

I was caught between a laugh and a blush when Detective Pitt came out to the lobby.

"What are you doing here?"

"We need to talk to you," I said, fully recovered from my earlier brain fog.

Detective Pitt glanced around to see who was watching and then escorted us back behind the security door into a conference room.

There was a bit of irony in the fact that the room he took us to was the same room that Jenna, Nana Jo, and I met with him in just a few months earlier when he'd been arrested for murder. The flush that went up his neck and made his ears inflamed told me that he was thinking of that same situation.

Inside, he quickly closed the door. "What are you doing here? I can't be seen helping you. I could lose—"

The door opened, and we never found out what he could lose. Detectives Fieldstone and Deevers sauntered into the room.

Detective Deevers glanced from me to Detective Pitt. "Isn't this cozy?"

"You're in for it now," Detective Fieldstone said. "Interfering with an active police investigation will cost you your badge."

Detective Pitt looked like a frightened rabbit. He opened his mouth, but before he could speak, the door flew open again.

Detective Pitt was standing in front of the door and was hit in the back when it opened.

Jenna blew in like a tornado. "What are you doing interrogating my client without legal counsel present?"

Detective Fieldstone was taken aback and stammered.

"We weren't interrogating your client," Detective Deevers said. "She came to us and was—" He halted when Jenna raised her hand.

"She's here because I instructed her to come," she said.

Detective Deevers frowned. "Why?"

"Because Mrs. Starczewski discovered a journal she *be-*

lieved belonged to Delia Marshall." Jenna extended her hand, and Nana Jo handed over the journal.

Jenna passed it to Detective Deevers.

Deevers and Fieldstone flipped through the journal.

"Where did she get this?" Detective Deevers asked.

"She was given a key to a post office box by a Bernie Goldberg. She had reason to believe the key was to Mrs. Marshall's post office box, but she wasn't certain until she got there and opened the box and saw Mrs. Marshall's name on some of the contents."

Detective Fieldstone's chest puffed, and he looked ready to explode. His partner put a calming hand on his arm.

"So, your client tampered with a crime scene and deliberately removed evidence—"

"Was Delia Marshall killed at the post office?" Jenna asked.

Silence.

Deevers plastered on a fake smile. "Counselor, surely you know that by removing this journal, there's no proof that the journal belonged to Delia Marshall, and if it did, she's broken the chain of evidence. Even if we wanted to use this journal in court, we couldn't."

"You interrogated Bernie Goldberg. He said he told you he had a key to Delia Marshall's post office box. Since you hadn't secured the contents, my client, Mrs. Starczewski, took it upon herself to deliver it to you. Frankly, you should thank her. If that really is evidence, it could have fallen into the hands of the *real* killer."

"Your sister is the *real killer*," Detective Fieldstone muttered.

"What was that, Detective?" Jenna glared.

Detective Fieldstone glared back but said nothing.

Since the other detectives arrived, Detective Pitt had been

as still as a deer in headlights. He made the mistake of moving, and Detective Fieldstone latched onto him.

He pointed his finger in Detective Pitt's face and scowled. "I'm going to report you for interfering with my case."

Nana Jo chuckled.

Detective Fieldstone turned to Nana Jo. "What's so funny?"

"I just find it amusing that Detective Pitt was just lecturing us about tampering with police evidence and threatening to have us arrested when here you are threatening to arrest him."

Detective Deevers frowned. "Are you telling me Detective Pitt wasn't helping you?"

"Pshaw." Nana Jo snorted. "Are you kidding? He tried to arrest my granddaughter, her assistant, her stepfather, and me. Do you really believe he'd try to help us?"

Deevers sucked his jaw. "Isn't that how he got shot? Helping you?"

"He got shot doing his job, serving and protecting the citizens of North Harbor," Jenna said. "He was shot apprehending a killer."

"Yeah, and he certainly holds a grudge," Nana Jo said. "He brings up the fact that he was shot every time we see him."

"So, you're telling me Detective Pitt hasn't been helping you by leaking department information to you?" Detective Fieldstone asked.

"What information do you think he's leaked?" I pulled out a notepad and pen.

Detective Fieldstone glared for a few more moments, but eventually, his shoulders went down a quarter-inch, and he sighed.

Jenna stood and glanced from Detective Fieldstone to Detective Deevers. "Now, if there's nothing else, we'll be leaving."

Detective Deevers gave a slight nod, and Jenna opened the door.

Irma, Dorothy, and Ruby Mae hurried out. Nana Jo was next.

As I was about to leave, Detective Fieldstone pounded his fist on the table and fixed me with an evil stare. "I don't care how many influential friends you have. You're guilty, and I'm going to bring you down if it's the last thing I do."

I've seen my sister angry many times, but never like this. I could have sworn there was smoke coming out of her ears. I was close enough to see her nostrils flare. Like a two-headed dragon, she turned to Fieldstone and spewed fire. "If you ever threaten my family again, I can guarantee you that it *will* be the last thing you do."

Chapter 16

Outside, Jenna marched to her car. She got in, backed out, and sped off without a word.

Nana Jo turned to me. "You think she's angry?"

I got into my car and laid my head on the steering wheel. "She's going to kill me and then eat me."

Nana Jo patted my back. "Your sister is like a cat. She's going to torture you first. Then she'll kill you."

I turned to stare at my grandmother. "Was that supposed to be comforting? Because it wasn't."

"It's supposed to shock you out of your pity party. Did it work?"

I sat up and stuck my tongue out.

"Good, now let's go see if we can't figure out what Delia Marshall was up to."

I drove back to the bookshop.

Inside, we went to the conference room. Nana Jo forwarded the pictures she took with her phone of Delia's journal. I stared at the pictures until my eyes crossed. "I'm going to print these out. Does anyone else want a printout?"

Ruby Mae and Dorothy raised their hands, but Irma and Nana Jo preferred to look at the images on their phones. I suspected Irma was texting one of her boyfriends, but that was fine. She'd uncovered a big clue. She deserved a break.

Snickers and Oreo followed me to my office and waited while I made three copies of the pictures.

Looking at the images as printouts didn't help, and after two hours, I was still confused.

"Well, we know she was trying to hide something, and this is her code," Nana Jo said.

"Yeah, but in order to break a code, don't you need some kind of key?" Dorothy asked.

"According to this cute young man I found surfing the web, you should look for single-letter words," Irma said. "He says they're almost always *I* or *A*."

I mentally apologized for thinking she wasn't engaged in finding the answer. "That's right, Irma. I did a bit of research about ciphers for one of my books. The most common letter is *E*. Look for repeating letter patterns. Those are often *TH* and *SH* or double letters, probably *Ls*."

"I've been focused on the smaller words," Ruby Mae said. "I figured the two-letter words would be easy."

"That's a good point." I smiled at Ruby Mae. "How's everyone doing?"

Grumbles in response.

Nana Jo stood up and stretched. "I'm not coming up with anything."

The others had nothing to add.

I yawned. "Neither am I. But I think it's a book cipher. I just don't know what book she used."

"Well, I've got a crick in my neck, and I think I'm going to do a bit more research."

"What kind of research?"

"I think we need to know more about Delia Marshall," Nana Jo said. "I'm going to talk to Freddie and see what I can find out. Can you give us a lift back to Shady Acres?"

"Sure. With the bookshop still closed by the police, I don't have anything else to do."

"They're keeping the bookstore closed out of spite. There's no reason why they need to keep the store closed."

"That really burns my butt," Irma said.

"It's an abuse of power, and that burns mine, too," Ruby Mae said. "I sure wish Daryl was here. He'd wipe that smug look right off Detective Fieldstone's face, and he would make them open the bookshop back up."

Daryl Stevenson was one of Ruby Mae's extended family, a great-nephew, who also just happened to be the acting chief of police for North Harbor.

"Where is Chief Stevenson?" Dorothy asked.

"Washington, D.C. There's a special meeting. Police chiefs from around the country are all there meeting with a special senate committee on crime." She smiled. "I'm so proud."

"You should be," Nana Jo said.

It didn't take long to drive to the Shady Acres Retirement Village. It was a community specifically for active seniors and had homes, condos, and apartments. Nana Jo bought a single-family home with views of Lake Michigan. Dorothy, Irma, and Ruby Mae had condos.

Nana Jo's words stuck with me, and I found myself pondering them over and over again. On the ride home, I tried to think of what I knew about Delia Marshall, other than the fact that she extorted money out of people. She used her platform as a weapon against those who didn't yield to her demands. And she abused animals . . . well, "abuse" may be too strong. After all, Snickers did lunge at her, but she wouldn't have lunged if Delia hadn't provoked her. Her mistreatment of my dogs was enough to establish my opinion of her. But was there more about her that we didn't know? Surely she had some redeeming qualities.

Back at the bookshop, I knew I should take advantage of this time while the store was closed to reorganize my bookshelves, dust, take inventory, anything. However, walking through the empty aisles made me sad. I tried not to head down the dead-end street of What-Ifs. *What if* we didn't find Delia's killer by the end of the week? *What if* Detective Fieldstone arrested me? *What if* my publisher found out and canceled my book? *What if* my publisher didn't cancel my book and readers found out that I was arrested for murder and refused to buy my book or gave me all one-star reviews?

Snickers got on her back legs and used my leg as a scratching post.

"Ouch!" I glared down at her.

She stretched and then walked over to her food dish.

"You've had your breakfast, but I suppose a snack wouldn't hurt." I opened the bag of all-natural dog chews that smelled awful but kept the poodles busy for the fifteen minutes it took them to devour them.

Generally, the treats were a great distraction while I wrote, so I took this as a hint. I needed something to keep my mind busy.

The servants' dining hall in Windsor Castle was a long, narrow space with a massive fireplace in the middle of the room and a long rectangular table surrounded by chairs. The layout was similar to practically every dining hall in great homes across England. The main difference was Windsor Castle's servants'

dining room was more of everything. It was longer. Larger. Narrower.

Thompkins lingered near a large marble table that was used as a buffet and admired the goodie-laden table while keeping a watchful eye on the Marsh servants. When the Marshes' servants first arrived at Windsor Castle, Thompkins was concerned that their excitement at seeing the royal family might cause them to misbehave and prove an embarrassment to the Marshes. However, he need not have worried. Everyone from Mrs. McDuffie to the footmen had been paralyzed with fear. Thompkins had drilled them on royal protocol so that even Gladys, the least coordinated of the bunch, was able to curtsy as if she'd served in the royal court her entire life. Preparing for the christening in an unfamiliar environment had them all too busy for nerves.

The Marshes' maid, Daisy, flopped down into a chair. "I'm plumb worn-out from running up and down those stairs. How do you manage to do that all day?"

Cora hadn't been at Windsor long, but you never would have known by the way she acted, especially in front of the servants. She smiled and poured Daisy a cup of tea before topping her own. "You learn to be efficient to prevent multiple trips."

"Plus, it keeps your legs in great shape," Maggie, a flirtatious young maid with dark hair, green eyes, and a Welsh accent, said, extending her leg to show its shapeliness.

Godfrey took a sip of tea. "Windsor's more than five hundred and ninety thousand square feet."

"Good Lord, that's massive," Flossie said. "I thought Wickfield Lodge was large when I first started in service with the Marshes, but this place is enormous. How on earth can you get about a place this big?"

Bobby, a freckle-faced footman with red curly hair, smiled. "Tunnels."

"What?" Flossie asked. "You mean to tell me in addition to all that space above ground, there's even more underground?"

"Not just underground. There are priest holes and secret passages the monarchs used for hiding in case of revolution." Bobby smiled at Flossie.

"The monarchs aren't the only ones that used those passages," Cora said.

"What do you mean?" Gladys's eyes grew larger, and she leaned toward Cora.

Cora glanced down the table at the housekeeper before adding, "I've seen the queen's lady-in-waiting, that Lady Redding, sneaking out through those tunnels."

"Why?" Gladys asked. "She's not a servant. She can come and go as she pleases. Can't she?" Maggie glanced around to make sure Mrs. McDuffie wasn't listening as she might take offense. She was a tough old bird and wouldn't take kindly to maids talking out of school.

Maggie grinned. "Why do you think, you silly goose? She's going to meet her fella."

"What fella? Who'd want that sour-faced old cow?" Gladys asked.

Maggie snickered. She looked around. No one appeared to be paying attention to their conversation, although the Marshes' butler was standing nearby. But it was far too tempting to have someone to gossip with for Maggie to stop now. Besides, Thompkins was the Marsh butler, not the king's butler. He couldn't sack her. "She's been sneaking out with the king's private secretary, Clive Elliott."

The revelation had the desired effect on Gladys, who stared open-mouthed for several seconds. "Well, you wouldn't catch me sneaking through no tunnels. I'll bet it's full of rats and spiders and all kinds of horrible critters." She shivered.

The conversation reverted back to the size of the castle and the challenges of cleaning it, so Thompkins slowly sauntered farther down the buffet until he was behind the two housekeepers.

"It's almost a thousand years old, too," Mrs. Jordan, the Windsor housekeeper, said.

If Thompkins were honest with himself, he would admit that the housekeepers were his biggest concern in coming here. Mrs. McDuffie was a hard worker and had a heart as big as the Thames, but she wasn't the most proper housekeeper. Lady Elizabeth was extremely tolerant of her less-than-perfect speech and occasionally impertinent behavior, but a proper housekeeper might not be as understanding. Thompkins wouldn't want to see Mrs. McDuffie's feelings hurt. However, he needn't have worried. Mrs. McDuffie and Mrs. Jordan hit it off immediately.

"My gracious," Mrs. McDuffie said. "That 'as to be 'ard on the maids to deal with an 'ouse this big and old. Fifty-two bedrooms is a lot of linens to change. Why, I don't know 'ow you manage."

"My word, yes," Mrs. Jordan said. "And that's just the royal and guest bedrooms. They've renovated some, but nothing like what you have at Wickfield Lodge." She leaned close. "Is it true you have one of those new iceboxes?"

Mrs. Anderson nodded. "Indeed. The Marshes have

added all of the latest conveniences. It certainly makes cooking a lot easier." She buttered a scone and therefore didn't see the looks that passed between the Marsh servants.

Thompkins slid down the table and glanced at his son-in-law, who was eagerly talking to one of the horologists hired to care for nearly 380 timepieces. This opportunity to come to Windsor Castle and meet the royal family was exciting, but Thompkins was also mindful of his responsibility to help His Majesty and, hopefully, bring a killer to justice. He moved next to the royal butler and sat down.

Thompkins coughed discreetly. "Terrible news about that young woman getting herself murdered in St. George's Chapel."

Godfrey took a sip of his tea. "Terrible indeed. His Majesty was terribly upset."

"Really?" Thompkins quietly sipped his tea.

"Why, of course he was upset," Godfrey said. "Who wouldn't be? What with that woman getting herself murdered and getting ahold of the documents."

Thompkins shrugged. "I suppose His Majesty must be more like his brother, the Duke of Windsor, than anyone knew."

A purple rage rose up, and Godfrey's eyes bulged. "What do you mean by that?"

Thompkins had judged the butler's loyalty and dedication accurately, but he had to play his hand carefully. He didn't want to alienate the butler. "Nothing. I didn't mean anything at all."

Godfrey took a deep breath. "You tell me what you meant."

"It's just that I'd heard rumors that when the

Duke of Windsor was king, that . . . well, that he liked to entertain Mrs. Simpson and would allow her to read from his red box. I just didn't believe that His Majesty, King George, would—"

"His Majesty would never willingly allow anyone to read his confidential dispatches." Godfrey's voice was getting louder, and a few of the servants who sat nearby had stopped to listen.

"Of course. I'm sorry. I meant no offense." Thompkins gave a slight bow of his head and sipped his tea.

Godfrey took a deep breath and then deflated like a balloon. He stared into his cup until he regained his control, and then turned to Thompkins. "It's not right. His Majesty is good. He's faithful to his wife, and he loves those girls. He never planned to be king . . . well, not for some time anyway."

Thompkins caught on to the butler's meaning and nodded. "You mean, if the Duke of Windsor had married and had children . . ."

Godfrey nodded. "Exactly. If he'd done his duty and married a proper wife, then his children would have succeeded him to the throne. But he was bewitched by that American temptress." He glanced around to make sure he wasn't overheard and then lowered his voice. "Anyway, King George knows his duty. He's doing a fine job, too. He and the queen consort traveling all over creation preparing for war." He shook his head. "He would never allow anyone to read his confidential papers."

"Then how?" Thompkins asked.

Godfrey gave a furtive look from left to right and then leaned closer. "I never did trust that squirrely private secretary of his."

"Clive Elliott?"

Godfrey nodded. "He's always skulking around the place and sneaking out with Lady Redding. You mark my words. That one's up to no good."

Thompkins did mark his words, but was this trusted butler simply shifting blame away from his master? Or did Clive Elliott really have a connection to Milicent Schmidt?

Lady Elizabeth sat in the ornately decorated drawing room of her cousin, Mary, the queen mother.

"Elizabeth, dear. How wonderful to see you again."

Lady Elizabeth and the queen mother chatted about distant and rarely seen relatives for several moments. Eventually, the women settled on a sofa near the fireplace.

When they were both caught up, Lady Elizabeth took a deep breath. She'd decided the direct approach would be best. Either her cousin would answer her questions or ask her to leave. She was banking on not getting tossed out of the castle. "Cousin Mary, what can you tell me about that woman who was murdered?"

"Nothing. I didn't know the woman."

Lady Elizabeth knew her cousin and suspected denial might be her first response and quickly moved to plan B. "I'm sure you didn't, but you're such a great judge of character, and I'm sure you weren't fooled by her for one second."

"You're absolutely right. In fact, I told Lucille that she was nothing more than a cheap piece of baggage not five minutes after I met her."

Flattery worked every time.

"What did she want?" Lady Elizabeth asked.

"Blackmail. That's the kind of woman she was. Thought she could get money out of—"

The queen mother realized she'd given herself away and clamped her mouth shut.

Lady Elizabeth nodded. "I thought as much. What did she have on poor David?" She paused, but the queen mother's lips were still closed. "Or was it the duchess that she'd managed to find dirt about?"

"Don't say that woman's name in my presence," the queen mother spat.

"What have David and Wallis done now? I thought they were safely tucked away in Paris?"

The queen mother sighed. "That's too close for comfort, if you ask me. He's too close to England and much too close to Germany. Bertie's going to need to move him out of Europe. I would suggest India, but *that woman* will have proclaimed herself empress? I'm thinking of one of the islands in the Caribbean. That nice Franklin Roosevelt promised he'd keep an eye on them."

"David will hate that," Elizabeth said. "He won't like being pushed out of the spotlight."

"Good. All the better."

"What did Milicent have on them?"

"I have no idea."

"Now, Mary—"

The queen mother held up a hand. "I never found out. She sent me a letter asking me to meet her in St. George's Chapel."

"Did you keep the letter?"

"Of course not. I burned it."

Lady Elizabeth sighed. "Pity. Well, what happened when you got to the chapel?"

"She was there and smiling like a cat that had gotten into the cream. She said unless I paid her some ungodly amount of money, she'd print a story in the papers that would ensure no one from the House of Windsor ever sat on the throne of England again."

Lady Elizabeth frowned. "And she gave no indication what this tremendous secret was?"

The queen mother shook her head. "None whatsoever. So, I turned to leave, and she grabbed my shawl. Can you believe that? She actually tore it."

"That explains how a piece of lace from your shawl was found in the dead woman's hand." Lady Elizabeth looked at her cousin. "What did you do with the rest of the shawl?"

The queen mother smiled. "I got rid of it."

Lady Elizabeth tried not to groan. "How?"

"I burned it along with the letter, which was a pity. That shawl was a gift from my goddaughter. But it was necessary. No one is going to threaten my son's right to rule and get away with it."

Lady Elizabeth closed her eyes and took several deep breaths.

"You don't look well," the queen mother said. "I know just what you need." She rose and walked to the wall and pushed a bell near the wall. "A cup of strong tea with lots of sugar, and you'll be back to yourself in no time."

Chapter 17

The doorbell rang and started the dogs barking, which pulled me out of the British countryside and back to the present.

One glance at the time, and I knew who was at the door.

Downstairs, I wasn't surprised to see Frank. "I'm sorry. I was writing, and I just got lost. Give me ten minutes, and I'll get dressed."

Frank pulled me close and kissed me. "We don't have to go out to dinner. I'm perfectly fine with staying in."

"Are you sure?"

He grinned. "Absolutely."

He let the dogs out, and I went upstairs, reapplied my makeup, and made myself more presentable.

Frank and the poodles made their way upstairs. "What do you have a taste for?"

"Where were we going?" Frank was a foodie who loved to experiment and try new things.

"I'm open. What strikes your fancy?"

"I need comfort food. Meat loaf or fried chicken and mashed potatoes." I shrugged. "But I can eat whatever."

He smiled. "I actually tried a new meat loaf recipe this morning. I can order dinner and have one of the waiters bring it over."

"Sounds wonderful."

He took out his cell phone and ordered, while I set the table.

After my late husband, Leon, died, I started buying paper plates, plastic silverware, and Styrofoam cups. Dining alone was a chore. Meals were something to be endured, not enjoyed. Frank had taught me that meals should be celebrated whether it involved a party of ten or a party of one. Now, I used the good china that previously only got brought out on Thanksgiving and Christmas, every day. Even if I was eating a burger and fries, removing the wrapper and plating them on good china elevated my burger and fries to another level. Surprisingly, I felt special, too. Sure, not using paper plates meant that I had a plate to wash, but that didn't take much effort. And all but the most delicate of china could stand a gentle cycle in the dishwasher.

Whether it was due to the fact that the order was placed by the owner or that the restaurant was less than half a block away, our food arrived quickly and was still steaming hot.

We talked and ate and enjoyed each other's company. Eating with Frank and hearing about his day was one of my favorite things about dating him. He truly believed in taking time to savor and enjoy the food and the conversation. Afterward, Frank and I washed and dried the dishes and then curled up together on the sofa. Snickers wasn't thrilled about sharing Frank's attention and curled up in his lap, leaving me very little room to snuggle. Oreo was content to lie on the sofa next to Snickers.

"How did things go?" Frank asked.

I shared the information we'd learned after he had left, as well as the details about the post office and Detectives Fieldstone and Deevers. I could tell he wasn't thrilled by the way he clenched his jaw whenever I mentioned either of the detectives.

"I've got a special recipe for ghost pepper chili I'd love to serve those two detectives that's guaranteed to change their outlooks on life."

"Ghost peppers? Aren't those super hot?"

He chuckled. "Yeah. When I was in the military, one of my buddies got some of the juice on his hands and forgot and wiped his eyes. Man, you should have heard him scream."

I gave him a playful punch. "That's cruel. You shouldn't laugh."

He continued to chuckle. "It was hilarious."

I snuggled up close to Frank. I could feel his strength. I didn't realize I was crying until the first tears fell.

Frank pulled me close. "What's wrong? You know it was just fun. He wasn't hurt. They flushed out his eyes with a saline solution and apart—"

I waved a hand to halt the words of explanation. "I know you'd never laugh if someone was seriously hurt. I don't know what's wrong with me. I guess . . . I was just thinking how nice this is, just sitting here with you. And then I started thinking, what if I get arrested and go to jail, and we can't get married, and we never get to—"

Frank kissed me silent. When we came up for breath, he looked into my eyes. "That isn't going to happen. We will figure out who killed Delia Marshall. We will get married. And we will have many evenings together."

I buried my head in his chest. With his arms wrapped around me, I felt loved and protected. Nothing bad could happen to me as long as we were together. "Nana Jo had a good idea."

"What's that?"

"She said we don't really know much about Delia Marshall as a person. We know she blackmailed people. But we don't really know anything about her. She left to meet with Freddie to see what he could find out."

"I might be able to help with that. I know someone who has access to . . . let's just say, he's got access to information." He glanced at his watch. "He's a few time zones away, so I should probably wait until the morning, but I'll get in touch with him first thing tomorrow and have him send me everything he can find."

"That's great. Maybe he could check on everyone? Martha Chiswick, Evelyn Randolph, Denver Benedict." I paused. "And maybe Preston Kincaid. He's the guy whose career Delia ruined."

Frank jotted the names down. "Got it."

"You know, I think I'm going to have a talk with the North Harbor librarian, Charlotte Simmons. She just may be able to help us."

Frank and I talked about our plans until he got a call. He glanced at the phone and then rolled his eyes.

"Who is it?" I asked.

"My mother."

I sat up. "You should take that."

He grinned mischievously. "I can think of something I'd rather do instead." He reached for me, but I dodged.

"No way. How do you know it isn't important?"

"This is more important." He kissed me.

I pulled away and gave him a playful swat. "Oh no. You call your mother."

"Are you serious?"

"Yes."

He gazed at me for several moments, but eventually pulled out his phone and redialed. "Hi, Mom. Sorry, I was . . . in the shower."

Liar, I mouthed.

"Everything's fine." He listened. "Well, I know for a fact that Sam would love to meet you, too."

I rolled my eyes.

"I don't know. She's pretty busy right now. Maybe in a couple of weeks . . . Well, I'll have to ask her. . . . She's . . . yes . . . I'm sure she'd love for you to come to North Harbor for a visit. We'd both love for you to come." He closed his eyes. "I'll talk to Sam and find out what date works. . . . Labor Day? Well, I don't . . . sure. I'll . . . okay, we'll talk tomorrow. I love you, too." He hung up.

"She's coming for Labor Day?"

He nodded. "I knew I shouldn't have answered."

"If I get out of this mess, I'll gladly entertain your mother for Labor Day. Scout's honor." I held up three fingers.

He grinned. "After a week with my mother, you might prefer prison."

Before I could respond, his phone rang again. This time it was the restaurant. There was a problem, and he had to leave.

We lingered over our good-byes, and then he left.

I let Snickers and Oreo out to take care of business. I couldn't help but glance at the dark lights over the garage apartment where my assistant, Dawson Alexander, stayed. I missed him. I hadn't been blessed with children, and Dawson was like the son I never had. I refused to allow thoughts that I might never see him again to take root in my brain. I knew they weren't true. Even in the worst-case scenario, Dawson would visit me in prison. Despite all of the terrible things his father had done to him over the years, he still visited him whenever he was locked up, which was usually at least once or twice each year. Instead, I decided to go back inside and write.

If my Nana Jo was right, and she usually was, and writing allowed my subconscious to sort through the clues and figure

out things my conscious mind couldn't, then I needed to
write. I needed all of the help I could get.

Lady Elizabeth sat on a sofa in the king's drawing
room. She pulled out her knitting, took a moment to
find her spot in the pattern, and then let her fingers
get busy. When she was comfortable, she looked up.
"Now, who wants to go first?"

Detective Inspector Peter Covington sat up. "The
coroner confirmed that Milicent Schmidt died from a
blow to the head with a blunt object."

"Did he have any idea of what type of weapon?"
Lady Elizabeth asked.

The detective inspector shook his head. "The
weapon wasn't found."

"Anything else?" Lady Elizabeth asked.

"They didn't find any fingerprints. The area had
been wiped clean."

"Isn't that odd?" Lord Browning asked.

"Not really. Most everyone knows that fingerprints can be used to identify them, so they wipe
them off." Detective Inspector Covington sighed.
"Crime writers are making the policeman's job a lot
harder." He flipped through a small notepad. "That's
about it. I wish I had more information."

"Actually, you've given us quite a good bit of information." Lady Elizabeth smiled.

"I'd like to know what that was?" Detective Inspector Covington frowned. "It seemed like worth-
less information to me."

"The murderer must have come prepared to kill the poor woman. He or she brought their own weapon and took it away when they left." Lady Elizabeth finished a difficult pattern, counted her stitches, and then glanced up. "Also, since there were no fingerprints found at the scene, then you've helped us confirm what Bertie . . . ah, I mean King George and the queen mother said."

"The queen mother?" Lady Daphne said. "You talked to Cousin Mary? I always knew you were brave, but . . ."

"I had tea with the queen mother." Lady Elizabeth smiled and then shared what she'd learned.

Detective Inspector Covington stared at Lady Elizabeth. "You mean to tell me she deliberately destroyed evidence? That's illegal."

Lady Clara chuckled. "I'd like to see you try to arrest her for it."

Lord William puffed on his pipe. "Went to my club today. I had a talk with Fordham-Baker."

"Oh, good," Lady Elizabeth said. "I was afraid maybe he wouldn't be there."

"He was there. There just about every day, or so I was told. Likes to sit in a chair near the window and close to the bar." Lord William refilled his pipe, dropping tobacco on his coat. "He knew Milicent Schmidt. Apparently, she had a habit of dropping hints that she knew something in the hopes that the person would confess and volunteer the information."

"Who would do something like that?" Lady Clara asked.

"You'd be surprised." Lord William lit his pipe and took several puffs before continuing. "She said everyone had secrets, and if she pretended she knew what it was and was on the verge of revealing it, then she often got a number of stories that way." He frowned. "Fordham-Baker suspected she was using a bit of blackmail, too. But he couldn't prove it."

"That lines up with what I found out," Lady Clara said. She turned to Lord William. "I'm sorry to interrupt. I can wait my turn."

"It's okay. I didn't find out anything else from him. Ran into an old buddy from the war office. I mentioned some of the people. The only names he knew were Lieutenant Jamison and his wife, Alice. His biggest frustration was that so many Brits have ties to Germany. Lieutenant Jamison's wife was the daughter of a prominent German merchant and a relative of Rudolf Hess." He puffed. "With war looming over us, it's going to make it bloody hard to know who to trust."

Lady Elizabeth paused her knitting and looked at her husband. "That's true, but surely he doesn't suspect that anyone so close to the royal family would be allied to Germany?"

"I don't believe it," Lady Penelope said. She hopped up from her seat and paced. "I mean, once Britain is at war, I can't believe anyone who has been born and raised here . . . a British citizen would deliberately betray their nation to their enemy."

"Sadly, some will knowingly and willingly betray their country, but the biggest issue is people who unknowingly give away secrets," Lord Browning said quietly.

Lady Penelope paused and turned to stare at the duke. "I don't understand. How can you unknowingly give away secrets?"

The duke smiled. "A cousin you've known your entire life writes and says they heard young Robbie has joined the armed forces. How is he doing? Aunt Minnie innocently responds that she's worried sick and frantically searching for warm socks and long underwear to help him get through the cold winters. You'd be surprised how quickly someone could find Robbie's last name and figure out troop movement."

Lady Penelope gasped and flopped back down in her seat. "Surely, no one would report that to the military and act on it. Would they?"

"As the Americans say, 'Loose lips sink ships,'" Lord Browning said.

Lady Daphne looked at her husband. "But so many people have friends and relatives in Germany. Even . . ."

Lord Browning reached out and squeezed his wife's hand.

Lady Elizabeth looked up from her knitting. "It's true. We have German relatives, but so does the king. It was only twenty-two years ago that the family changed their name from Saxe-Coburg-Gotha to Windsor, which is why it's vital that we figure out who murdered that woman. With the nation on the brink of war, it's imperative that the nation has a leader that they can trust. Now isn't the time to have people questioning the royal family." She turned to her husband. "Were you able to find out anything else, dear?"

Lord William shook his head.

"Who wants to go next?" Lady Elizabeth glanced around the room.

Lady Daphne raised a hand. "I had tea with Cousin

Lucille. I listened to gossip about everyone from the fendersmith to the scullery maid."

"Fendersmith?" Detective Inspector Covington said. "What's that?"

"The person who tends the fireplaces," Lady Elizabeth said. "I believe there are more than three hundred in the castle."

Detective Inspector Covington gave a low whistle.

"But did she know anything about Milicent Schmidt?" Lady Clara asked.

"When I finally steered the conversation to the murder, she claimed she didn't know anything about it," Lady Daphne said. "Lady Lucille Redding is a snob. She acted as though the murder of a journalist was beneath her. She complained about all of the servants. Well, she complained about practically everyone, including the queen, the queen mother, and King George the Sixth. Do you know she actually criticized King George the Fifth for dying at such an *inconvenient* time?"

"He could hardly choose his time of death," Lord Victor Carlston said.

Lady Daphne shook herself. "She's such a negative person, I loathe talking to her, but there was something different about her. . . ."

"How do you mean?" Lady Elizabeth asked.

"She seemed . . . happy."

"I'm afraid I don't know your cousin, but is that so unusual?" Lord Browning said. "She sounds like one of those spiteful cats that love to gossip, and now she had someone new to bore with her complaints." He lit his pipe and stretched his legs in front of the fire.

"It wasn't like that," Lady Daphne said. "It was as though she had some secret delight." She chuckled.

"If I didn't know better, I might suspect that Cousin Lucille was in love."

"Unreal. I'll never believe it."

When the clamor from the younger women of the Marsh family died down, Thompkins coughed discreetly and stepped forward.

"Yes, Thompkins?" Lady Elizabeth said.

"Actually, Lady Browning's report matches what I heard in the servants' hall today," Thompkins said.

The butler shared what he'd learned from Godfrey and the conversation he overheard between the maids Gladys and Maggie.

Lady Clara smiled. "Well, what do you know about that? Cousin Lucille and Clive Elliott are a couple."

"I knew something was going on with her. She was absolutely giddy. I chalked most of her excitement up to having someone to listen to her gossip, but whenever I've been trapped . . . I mean, spoken to her in the past, she's never been this gleeful. Her cheeks were rosy, and her eyes were bright. She was almost . . . attractive."

"Now, Daphne, Lucille is a bit plain, but she's intelligent, and she volunteers a lot of time to helping orphans and the poor," Lady Elizabeth reminded her niece. She then looked around. "Anyone else?"

"Sorry, but Claire can't meet with me until tomorrow," Lady Clara said. "She said she had to meet with a source about a story she's working on, and if she misses her deadline, her editor will have her guts for garters."

"That's perfectly all right," Lady Elizabeth said.

"I'm afraid Penelope and I are both a bust today, too," Victor said. "But we're having lunch with Lieutenant Jamison and his wife, Alice, tomorrow."

"Excellent. I think we have enough to think about for one day anyway."

Lord Browning frowned. "For the life of me, I can't imagine what we've learned other than that the queen's lady-in-waiting is probably having a fling with the king's private secretary."

Lady Elizabeth finished the row she was knitting. "We've learned that the murder was probably premeditated. The killer brought their own weapon, wiped away all of the fingerprints, and took the murder weapon with them. Since neither the king nor the queen mother's fingerprints were found at the scene, then the murder probably happened *after* they visited with Milicent Schmidt."

Detective Inspector Covington leaned forward. "Wait, how can you be sure of that? Either one of them could have wiped their fingerprints away, just like anyone else."

"True, but I suppose it goes back to human nature," Lady Elizabeth said.

"I don't understand."

Thompkins coughed and stepped forward. "If you will permit me, I believe I can explain."

Lady Elizabeth smiled and gave a slight nod for the butler to continue.

"Both the queen mother and King George are accustomed to a lifestyle of privilege. They're accustomed to having people clean up after them."

Lady Elizabeth nodded. "Exactly. Neither of them would even think to wipe their fingerprints from the scene."

Detective Inspector Covington ran a hand through his hair. "You're probably right, but I don't know that your explanation would hold up in a court of law." He snapped his fingers. "What about the lace found in the dead woman's hand?"

"Milicent Schmidt had to have been alive to tear the shawl," Lady Elizabeth said. "Plus, I can't believe the queen mother would have brought a weapon, hit and killed Milicent Schmidt, and then taken the weapon." She paused. "Some of it is character, as Thompkins mentioned, but some of it is logic. The queen mother wouldn't have killed Milicent without first finding out what she knew. If Milicent knew something that could prevent a Windsor from ever sitting on the throne of England, she would want to find out what that secret was, so she could put an end to the threat."

"How do you know she didn't find out before she killed her?" Detective Inspector Covington asked.

Lady Elizabeth smiled. "The queen mother may not care for Wallis, the Duchess of Windsor, but she loves David. She wouldn't try sending him to the Caribbean if the threat was . . . what's the word? Neutralized."

Lord Browning nodded. "So, you believe her when she said she never found out the truth?"

Lady Elizabeth thought for a few moments. "Yes. I believe her."

"Then so do I," Lord Browning said. "We'd better get busy. We only have two days until the christening."

~~~~

Wednesday, I woke up with a renewed determination. Like Lady Elizabeth, I had come to a few conclusions based on human nature. Delia Marshall had a blackmailing/extortion scheme that had been working for her. She'd been blackmailing Evelyn Randolph, Martha Chiswick, and Denver Benedict for years, and she'd never been killed. What was different about this time? Why would Evelyn Randolph risk killing Delia Marshall now? She could have waited until her soon-to-be-late husband was dead. And what was the story behind the exposé that she and Martha Chiswick were working on? Maybe Delia found out about it and threatened to expose their secrets? Evelyn's secret could have cost her her life if her husband found her. Denver Benedict's secret could have stripped him of his awards and his reputation. It would, I think, have ruined any chance he had of ever publishing again, but I would need to talk to an expert. So, I made a mental note to call my agent.

In fact, there's no time like the present. I hopped out of bed, grabbed my cell phone, and dialed while I walked downstairs to let the dogs out.

"You're up bright and early this morning," Pamela Porter said.

My agent, Pamela Porter, was a middle-aged Black woman. She was also another member of Ruby Mae's extensive family network. She'd been a publisher for twenty years before she decided to start her own literary agency, Big Apple Literary Agency. She called her company a *boutique agency*. Which I'd learned basically means small, pretty much a one-woman show. However, she was nice, direct, and tough as nails. We hit it off immediately, and I trusted her and valued her insight.

I glanced at the time. "I'm sorry. I had no idea it was so early. Did I wake you?"

"Not at all. I'm up at five thirty every morning. So, I'm just going through my slush pile of queries looking for the next Samantha Washington that I can promote." She laughed.

"I have something to tell you." I spilled my guts about everything going on with Delia Marshall and the possibility that my book signing may happen from jail.

"I read that she died, and I can't say that there were too many people mourning her death," Pamela said.

"Please, if you know anything that can help me find anyone else who might have wanted to kill her, I would appreciate it."

"Publishing feels big, but in actuality it's a *very* small world. Everybody knows everybody else. An editor may have done an internship at one publishing house and then switched to another before finally landing at a third. Plus, everyone talks."

I felt that she was saying more than her words indicated. "Okaaay."

"If Delia Marshall threatened one author, no matter how much the author would want it to remain secret, chances are, they've told someone else. I can say that rumors have gone around, but no one could confirm anything. And no one wants to accuse someone of a crime like blackmail without proof."

"I can understand, but surely there was something that could be done."

She sighed. "Some of the newspapers had stopped carrying her column, but as small as the publishing world is, it's also very slow."

"Don't I know it. It's been over a year since I signed my contract, and my book hasn't been released yet."

"Exactly. Does that answer your question?"

"It does, but can I pick your brain about something?"

"Sure."

Without using names, I put forward a scenario involving an award-winning author whose work was later found to be fiction. "What type of repercussions could that bring? Would the writer be blacklisted?"

"The repercussions depend on the awards received. If it was a prestigious award like a Pulitzer, then it could be very devastating for a writer. It's hard to say if anyone would be willing to invest money in another book by that author."

We chatted a bit longer, but Pamela had work to do, and I had a murderer to catch.

Chapter 18

Nana Jo was sitting at the breakfast bar drinking coffee when I went back upstairs. "What are your plans?"

I glanced at my watch. "I'm going to head over to the North Harbor Library and have a talk with Charlotte Simmons. I'm hoping she can tell me about Delia's past."

"Good idea. Don't forget to ask her about the other suspects. Evelyn, Denver, and Martha were all members of the Mystery Mavens, but never underestimate the value of a librarian. They have resources you wouldn't believe."

"True. How about you? What are your plans?"

"I've got a friend at the newspaper. I'm going to see what she can tell me. I'm wondering if they knew about Delia's tactics."

"I sure hope not. That would be so disillusioning to know that people knew what Delia Marshall was doing and didn't do anything about it."

I took a shower, got dressed, gave the poodles a treat, and headed for the library.

North Harbor Library was a concrete and glass building that was built in the 1970s. It wasn't very distinctive. The door was propped open, so I snuck inside. The carpet had been ripped up from the flooding and the books and bookshelves removed, so it was a vast open space with concrete floors. There was a watermark on all of the walls that indicated how far the water had come, and there were large fans plugged in everywhere. Eventually, the water would be removed, but the damp, moldy smell would linger unless the drywall was removed and replaced.

I found Charlotte at a makeshift desk set up in the middle of the room.

"Samantha, how are you? I heard about Delia Marshall. I can't help feeling like it's my fault."

"Why?"

"If you hadn't volunteered to help us out, then Delia and the Mystery Mavens never would have come to your bookshop, and Delia might not have gotten herself murdered."

I hesitated. "You think her murder was somehow connected to my bookshop? Charlotte, I swear, I didn't have anything to do with Delia Marshall's murder."

She reached out and touched my arm. "Oh, I didn't mean . . . I'm sorry. I know you didn't have anything to do with Delia's death. I just meant it wouldn't have happened in your bookshop."

I thought about that for a few moments but decided to shake it off. "I didn't really know Delia, and so that's why I'm here."

"Of course, please tell me how I can help." She held out a hand, inviting me to sit.

I sat in the folding chair across from her. "I'm trying to make sense of this entire thing. Who wanted Delia Marshall dead? And it dawned on me that I didn't really know anything about her. I was hoping you could tell me something that might help me point the police in another direction."

"I guess the rumors are true." She smiled. "I'd heard you were a bit of an amateur sleuth."

"I have been able to assist the police with one or two of their investigations, but I certainly wasn't working alone."

"What do you want to know?"

"What kind of person was she?"

"I think the best word for Delia Marshall was...exacting. She wanted what she wanted, when she wanted it. I remember she had to have the exact edition of a book."

"What do you mean?" I asked.

"If she wanted a book, say, *Murder on the Orient Express*, she wanted a specific copy of the book. Once, she wanted *The Mysterious Affair at Styles,* but the edition she wanted was already checked out. Now, we have multiple copies of all of Agatha Christie's books and there were several copies of the book, but she refused. She had to have that one, specific edition by a particular publisher." She shook her head. "I have to say, there were times when she was rather trying. How was she with you?"

"I'll be honest, she was rude, obnoxious, and demanding when she came to my bookshop." I shared how Delia expected catered meals and even wanted to use my personal space rather than the meeting room.

Charlotte's mouth hung open in shock. After a few moments, she shook her head. "Sam, I'm so sorry. She was all of those things here, too, but frankly, I ignored her. I guess she thought since you're an author, she could throw her literary weight around and coerce you into giving her what she wanted." She pursed her lips. "That makes me furious to think that she would do that to you."

I took a minute to calm the librarian, who had turned red and genuinely looked distressed.

Eventually, Charlotte sat back and thought for a few moments, and then she smiled and quickly started typing on her computer. "I hate how complicated things have become with passwords. Uppercase, lowercase, numbers, special characters, you can't reuse passwords that you've used in the past six months, no real words. I mean, how are you supposed to remember them all?"

"I know what you mean. I struggle to remember what I had for dinner. Every system has a password, and then they make you change them every month or two. It's frustrating. I mean, I know why they do it, but it's virtually impossible to keep track of them all."

"Exactly, I had to start writing them all down. I keep a notebook with all of my passwords in it." She held up a small journal that looked similar to the journal we'd found in Delia Marshall's post office box. "I can't let our technology guy know I have this because he would have a heart attack, but it's the only way I can keep up with them all."

"Excuse me, but where did you get that journal?" I asked. "I think Delia Marshall had one just like that."

She turned the journal over and I saw that it had the name of Evelyn Randolph and Martha Chiswick's book on the back. "Evelyn and Martha had a ton of them made. . . . I guess I got it from them." She shrugged. After a few moments, she smiled again. "I didn't know Delia on a personal level, but I've always said you can tell a lot about a person by the books they read."

I felt dizzy from the topic changes but nodded my agreement.

She tapped a bit more, then turned to me and said, "Library records are private. Without a subpoena, I can't share any information with you."

"Okaaay, but she's dead."

"It doesn't make any difference." She smiled, stood, and picked up her coffee mug. "I'm going to the back . . . waaay in the back to get some coffee. It should take about five minutes. Would you like coffee?"

"No, thank you."

Her gaze moved from me to her computer screen and then to her notebook, and then she winked at me.

I gave a brief nod.

"It was such a pleasure chatting with you. Please come back again sometime." She smiled, turned, and walked out.

As soon as she turned the corner, I slid over in front of her screen. One glance at her notebook showed her username and password, which I entered into the screen she had left up on the computer. It took me into the library's computer system. It didn't take long to figure out how to look up Delia's library history. I pulled an envelope and a pen out of my purse and quickly jotted down everything on the screen. As a mystery reader and reviewer, most of her choices weren't surprising, but there was one item that puzzled me. But I didn't have time to analyze it, so I scribbled down as much information as I could. I was tempted to pull up my own history but five minutes wasn't very much time, so I squelched the feeling and left as quickly as I could.

I got in the car and drove home with just enough time to meet Nana Jo and walk down the street to Frank's for our noon meeting.

Upstairs, I took my same seat. Everyone was present except Detective Pitt, and I wondered if he was still upset about the journal, but he rushed up the stairs just as Nana Jo was taking out her iPad.

"Glad you were able to make it," Nana Jo said. She smiled at the detective, who merely grunted as he plopped down in his seat. She glanced around the room. "Now, who wants to go first?"

I raised my hand and shared the conversation I'd had with the North Harbor librarian.

"I'm not sure I understand how the books she reads are going to help," Detective Pitt said.

"Since I started working at the bookstore with Sam, I feel like I know a lot about people based on the types of books they buy," Nana Jo said. "People who like to cook usually like culinary mysteries, and people who are into crafts look for knitting or quilting mysteries."

"Knitting mysteries?" Detective Pitt said.

"Don't knock it until you've tried it," I said. "There's generally some type of mystery for everyone."

"And what did you learn about Delia Marshall?" Nana Jo asked.

"She checked out a lot of Agatha Christie books." I glanced down at the items I'd scribbled down on the envelope. "But . . . it's weird."

"What's weird about that?" Nana Jo said. "You LOVE Agatha Christie."

"I know, and like me, Delia rereads the same books, but . . . There's just something a bit odd about how often she rereads the same books."

"Why would anyone reread a mystery after they've already read it once?" Detective Pitt asked.

"I often reread books," I said.

"I reread some books, too," Jenna said. "But I have to agree with Detective Pitt here. I seldom reread mysteries. Once you know whodunit, what's the point?"

"Well, as a writer, I reread books, especially Agatha Christie, to see *how* she did things. How she put the clues and the red herrings in the book." I frowned. "But Delia Marshall wasn't a writer . . . at least, I don't think she was."

"Was that it?" Dorothy asked. "Were Agatha Christie the only books?"

"No, she also had asked for a copy of a thesis novel from someone named Chuck Nobles," I said.

"Chuck Nobles?" Nana Jo asked.

"Yeah, do you know him?"

"Who's Chuck Nobles, and what's a thesis novel?" Irma asked.

"When you get a graduate degree like an MFA or a PhD, you have to write a thesis or dissertation," I said. "It's an original work that the student has to write and defend in order to graduate. So, this Chuck Nobles must have written a thesis, and it's in an archive somewhere at the university library where he graduated."

"Why would Delia want to see it?" Jenna asked.

"That's what makes it unusual," I said. "After someone graduates, these documents are largely forgotten."

Nana Jo tapped her pen. "Now I remember why that name sounded familiar. Chuck Nobles was the name used in the book by Evelyn Randolph and Martha Chiswick that I told you about. The guy in the story who was murdered."

Something was starting to float around in my brain, but for the life of me, I couldn't figure out how to connect the dots.

After we exhausted the conversation, Nana Jo asked who wanted to go next, and Jenna raised her hand.

"I haven't found out much, but I did learn that the governor is planning to appoint Judge Ethan Chiswick to the state supreme court."

"Chiswick as in Martha Chiswick?" Dorothy asked.

Jenna nodded. "Her husband. He's a really nice man. I've tried several cases in front of him, and he's always fair."

"I wonder if Delia knew something about Martha or her husband that Martha wouldn't have wanted made public?" Ruby Mae asked.

"That's not all." Jenna glanced around and leaned close. "My source also said that Judge Chiswick is taking Preston Kincaid as his aide."

Frank's cell phone rang. He glanced at the phone, got up, and walked to a private corner to take the call. After a few moments, he came back over to the table. "Sorry to interrupt, but I just learned that Martha Chiswick and her husband are at the airport in Chicago trying to take a plane to Mexico."

"What? How are they leaving the country?"

Frank held up a hand to halt all of the questions we were firing at him. "Do you want me to stop them from leaving the country?"

Everyone turned to stare at me.

"Can you do that?" I asked.

"I can't, but my friend can." Frank smiled and held up his phone.

"Yes, I mean . . . I didn't think murder suspects would be allowed to leave the country," I said.

Jenna took a deep breath. "They wouldn't, but Deevers and Fieldstone are too focused on Sam as the killer that they aren't looking at anyone else."

I turned to Detective Pitt. "How do we tell them that Martha Chiswick is trying to leave the country?"

"I can call them and tell them that I heard two of their suspects were trying to skip town," he said.

"I don't want you to get in trouble. I mean, I don't want this to get back to them that you were involved."

"We can call and leave an anonymous message," Irma said.

"But they'll know who you are," Ruby Mae said. "They'll be able to trace your phone number."

"We can use my burner phone," Nana Jo said. She reached in her purse and pulled out a cell phone.

When the shock wore off, I leaned across and whispered to Jenna, "When did our grandmother get a burner phone? And why does she need a burner phone?"

"I don't even want to know." Jenna waved over the server and asked for a glass of Moscato.

Detective Pitt gave Frank the telephone number, and he called and left an anonymous tip. When he was done, he sat back down next to me and asked, "Why does your grandmother have a burner phone?"

I shook my head.

"Attempting to flee the country should be enough to convince those two bozos that they need to look at someone other than Sam," Nana Jo said.

"We don't know why they're leaving," Detective Pitt said. "Maybe they cleared it with Deevers and Fieldstone first."

Frank got a text message. "They did *not* clear a trip to Mexico with Detective Deevers beforehand, and the Chiswicks have been detained."

We discussed the Chiswicks a bit, but Nana Jo quickly refocused us by asking for more reports.

Detective Pitt raised his hand. "After you all left, I decided to run the names of some of the other suspects through CODIS. I didn't think Deevers and Fieldstone were being thorough." He looked flush and avoided eye contact.

Jenna and I exchanged a quick glance. She'd noticed his discomfort, too. Although, I wasn't sure if his embarrassment was related to the way he had been treated earlier or the ineptitude of his fellow officers. Perhaps it reminded him of himself. After a few seconds, he cleared his throat and continued.

"Judge Ethan Chiswick is Martha's *second* husband. Her first husband was a conman named Wayne Kramer. He could have taught Delia Marshall a thing or two."

"Was he a blackmailer, too?" Ruby Mae asked.

Detective Pitt nodded. "Blackmail, extortion, fraud, wire fraud, embezzlement, you name it."

"Interesting, but . . . I don't see . . ." I stared at Detective Pitt, who smiled like a Cheshire cat.

"You don't see what Martha's first husband has to do with Delia Marshall?" He leaned back in his chair and smiled. "Notice, I called him her first husband and not her ex-husband."

It took a moment for me to grasp the importance of what he said. "Wait, you mean Martha Chiswick is a bigamist?"

Detective Pitt grinned and nodded.

"Could she be arrested for that?" I asked Jenna.

"In Michigan, it will depend on the circumstances, but she could, if she knew her first husband was alive and knowingly married someone else, then . . . she could be arrested and have to serve up to four years in prison."

"Martha Chiswick is a bigamist," Nana Jo said. "Delia Marshall must have found out about it and blackmailed her. Something like that wouldn't look good when Judge Ethan Chiswick is being considered for the state supreme court. Martha certainly had the motive to kill Delia Marshall."

"Attempting to flee the country certainly doesn't look good," Jenna said, and stood. "I'm going to do some research and then swing by the police station. I want to see the looks on Deevers's and Fieldstone's faces when they find out that someone else has a stronger motive than Sam to kill Delia." She left.

The atmosphere in the room was suddenly a lot lighter, and for the first time since this madness started, I felt hopeful.

"Well, I think this calls for a celebration," Nana Jo said. "Let's go to the casino and tie one on?"

"Hot da—"

"Irma!"

Irma burst into a coughing fit.

Frank leaned over. "I have to work, but you go and have a good time. You deserve to have some fun."

Our previously quiet group was a lot more jovial. Although something was tugging at the back of my mind. Still, I felt like a weight had finally been lifted.

We finished eating, and I promised to pick the girls up from the retirement village at eight.

Nana Jo and I walked home in good spirits. She grabbed Martha and Evelyn's book and went to her room. I tried to figure out what was bothering me, but it evaporated like smoke whenever I tried to pinpoint what was wrong. I hoped a bit of time writing might help me figure it out.

Lords Victor Carlston and James Browning walked past the Windsor Castle guards' room. Victor Carlston looked up as he caught sight of Lieutenant Jamison and a tall American dressed in the blue regimental uniform of the United States Air Force.

The American soldier came to an abrupt stop and saluted.

Victor and James snapped to attention and returned the salute.

The colonel was shorter and stockier than Victor, with dark hair and a friendly smile.

"Colonel Edge?" Victor said.

The colonel gave up his serious attitude and flashed a big smile that lit up his entire face. Victor extended his arm, and Colonel Edge pulled him into a big bear hug. "Captain Carlston, fancy meeting you here. I'm just getting a tour of this little castle from Lieutenant Jamison. Do you men know each other?"

Victor nodded and introduced his brother-in-law, and the two men shook hands.

"Normally, a good ole Southern soldier like myself would have taken offense at the term 'Yankee,' but I have to say that being here in England, I have a fairly good idea how that Connecticut Yankee must have felt in King Arthur's Court that Mark Twain wrote about." The colonel laughed.

"How do you two know each other?" Lieutenant Jamison asked.

Lord Victor Carlston smiled. "Back when the colonel was merely a lieutenant, during the war, I had a slight disagreement with a couple of soldiers," Victor explained.

The colonel leaned his head back and roared with laughter. "You Brits sure have the gift of understatement." He leaned toward Lieutenant Jamison. "This flyboy got tired of taking guff from this Russian officer and hauls back and knocks the man out cold. Well, the Russians all jumped in, and then the Brits and the Canadians got in on the brawl, and the next thing you know, there's a skirmish worse than anything going on the front lines." He laughed. "I was military police, and by the time I got the whole thing sorted out, the Boches were almost on top of us, and we had to skedaddle. Well, I don't know how it happened, but in the middle of the chaos, I got separated from my folks and ended up in an airplane with this hotshot."

Victor chuckled. "Since the lieutenant outranked me, and I might have still been under arrest, I got pushed into the back of a plane. We got up in the air, and that's when he started yelling for a bag."

"A bag?" Lieutenant Jamison asked. "Whatever for?"

Victor shook his head. "He was airsick."

Jamison stared at the colonel's uniform. "But you're in the air force."

Colonel Edge laughed. "I was just a naïve kid from a tobacco farm near Conway, South Carolina, when I joined the military. Heck, I was so wet behind the ears. I don't even know how I ended up in the line for the air force. My dad served in the navy, and I thought I was in the line for the navy." He laughed. "When I got to the front of the line, I saw that each branch of the military had different lines, and I'd been standing in the wrong one. By then, it was too late, so I just figured that must be where the Good Lord meant for me to be. Anyway, I started thinking I'd be one of those flying aces, even though I'd never even been in an airplane. When I finally did get up in the air, I was fine as long as I wasn't the one doing the flying. Once I got in the pilot's seat, I got airsick every dadgum time. When I found out this kid knew how to fly, I told him to get his fanny up there and fly this dad-blasted thing." He chuckled.

"It wasn't until later that I found out he'd only had five hours of solo flying," Victor said with a laugh. "If I'd known that, I probably would have taken my chances with the Germans."

Lieutenant Jamison casually glanced at his watch, and Colonel Edge got the message. "Well, I sure wish we had time to catch up on old times, but I'm still a working stiff. It looks like you've hung up your wings."

"For now," Victor said. "Perhaps you'll let me stand you a beer later?"

The men agreed. Lord Browning turned to Victor after Lieutenant Jamison and Colonel Edge were gone. "What is dadgum?"

Victor shrugged. "Beats me."

★ ★ ★

Later, Victor and Penelope left to dine with
Lieutenant Jamison, and James headed to Victoria
Barracks. Inside, he followed a small corridor to a
conference room. After a brief knock, he entered.
Inside, Colonel Edge turned and extended his hand in
greeting.

"James . . . or am I supposed to call you Lord Browning?" Colonel Edge said, grinning. "I was so shocked
to see you with Carlston, I just about gave everything
away."

"I've seen you in action, and I don't believe a
word of it." James sat. "But I didn't know you knew
Victor."

"I met him before I got shanghaied into all this
cloak-and-dagger black-bag stuff. Good man, young
Carlston. Does he know about your . . . activities?"

James shook his head. "Victor is a good man, and
I'd trust him with my life, but he hasn't been briefed.
He knows that I work with MI5 but isn't privy to the
details."

The colonel nodded. "Now, let's get the business
taken care of."

Even though it was just the two of them, they
both leaned close and spoke in low tones for several
minutes. After a quarter of an hour, the colonel
leaned back in his chair.

James pulled out a cigar. He offered one to
Colonel Edge.

The colonel took the cigar and sniffed it. He held
it between his fingers, but the colonel refused and
handed the cigar back when James extended his
lighter. "I would love to smoke that, but I promised
my wife I wouldn't."

James smiled. "How is Rebecca?"

Colonel Edge's eyes lit up. "Pretty as a sunrise over the Atlantic Ocean. I heard some little filly hog-tied you, too."

James grinned. "If by that you mean I'm happily married, then you're right. My wife's name is Daphne, and I couldn't be happier."

"Does *she* know what you do?"

"Most of it."

Colonel Edge nodded. "Shouldn't be secrets between married folk, but some things are best left unsaid. Now, I have a feeling you're here for more than just to get my report. Anything you can talk about?"

James took a long puff on his cigar. He briefly filled the colonel in on the journalist's murder, carefully leaving out any information that would implicate the royal family in her death. "I don't suppose you've come across anything that might help?"

To James's surprise, Colonel Edge folded his hands across his chest and stared in a manner that told the duke he did indeed know something that might help.

"Funny you should mention Milicent Schmidt. I believe your Lieutenant Jamison might have been one of the folks she tried her little blackmail game on."

James sat up. "What do you mean?"

"Well, part of the reason the military had Jamison showing me around was because he'd been approached by a woman . . . a journalist accusing him of misconduct in the sinking of HMS *Thetis*."

"*Thetis*? That was an accident. There was an investigation that cleared the navy of any misconduct. What evidence could she possibly have had?"

"None . . . at least that's what Jamison says. He claims he met Schmidt and they argued, but he refused to pay her, in his words, '*one bloody farthing.*' "

"What happened after that?"

"He claimed he stormed out. Said he left her sitting in the loft at St. Georges Chapel, laughing." He paused. "There's one curious point. According to Jamison, Schmidt was sitting in the church laughing like a hyena. Before he left, he thought he heard her singing a song about Alice. He said it stuck with him because his wife's name is Alice, but he was hotter than a wet hen and just kept on going."

"Do you believe him?"

"I don't know. He seems honest and straightforward, the kind of man who might kill if he were provoked. But he's also the kind of man who wouldn't lie. If he killed that woman, he'd own it."

"What's the American interest in all of this?"

"With things the way they are, the U.S. is curious when there's a rumor that someone with ties to the military and a close relationship to the king is getting a bit too cozy with the enemy."

Lord Browning sat up. "Who?"

"Our sources say that Lieutenant Jamison's wife, Alice, has been chummy with a fella by the name of Herbert von Dirksen, with the German Embassy."

"That's a serious accusation. What proof do you have?"

"Nothing concrete as yet, but we're keeping an eye on her . . . and her access to the royal family." He sighed. "Of course, it could be purely romantic. She might be having an affair, and the lieutenant may not be involved at all." He shook his head. "Never thought I'd see the day when adultery would be the lesser of the two evils."

"Anything tying Lieutenant Jamison to Dirksen?"

"Not that I've been able to find." Colonel Edge narrowed his gaze and leaned back. "What do you think?"

Lord James Browning took a pause. "Jamison was trained in covert ops by the best spies in the world. Lieutenant Jamison knows how to kill, and if threatened, he wouldn't hesitate to do it. If he killed Milicent Schmidt, he'd be able to lie in a way that no one would ever find out. I think Lieutenant Jamison is an extremely dangerous man."

Chapter 19

I sat up and stretched. Something I'd written struck a chord in my brain, but it was gone before I could put my finger on it.

"Sam, are you ready?" Nana Jo asked.

I glanced at my watch. It was later than I thought. So, I closed my laptop and shoved it in my bag, and got ready to go.

Nana Jo fed the poodles and took them outside while I freshened up. Once they were inside and tucked in with their nightly treats, we headed out.

The drive to Shady Acres Retirement Village was short and uneventful. I pulled up to the front of the building, and everyone piled into the back seat.

The drive to the Four Feathers Casino was also short and uneventful. The casino was owned by the Pontolomas, a Native American tribe indigenous to the area. The Pontolomas bought two hundred acres of land in the middle of nowhere and built an impressive casino that resembled ancient tribal lodges but on a much grander scale. I followed a winding path that meandered through woods full of deer, pheasants, coyotes, and black bears. The tribal police ensured that nothing dangerous ventured too close to the casino. Despite being in a small town, the Four Feathers was an impressive 150,000 square-foot resort built around a man-made lake. The resort included a five-hundred-room luxury hotel with three bars, seven restaurants, retail shops, and an event center that drew big-name entertainers from all over the world. Of course, there was also a casino.

I pulled up to the front of the casino and unloaded my passengers, and then I parked in the covered garage and walked inside. After my late husband's death and buying the bookshop, I started hanging out with my grandmother and her friends from the retirement village. Coming to the Four Feathers Casino became one of our regular hangouts. Nana Jo and the girls considered it clean, harmless fun. I agreed.

Our regular routine involved me parking the car while the others secured a seat at one of the restaurants. This was where Ruby Mae's connections came in handy. Regardless of the length of the lines, we never had a problem getting seated. Today was no different.

When I got to the buffet, I saw the gang sitting at a large table near the dessert table. One of Ruby Mae's grandsons, nephews, or great something or others was chatting with her while a woman dressed in a white chef's outfit stood nearby. I slid into the booth next to Nana Jo, who had already ordered me water with lemon.

The girls preferred the buffet to the casino's other restaurants because of the variety and speed. I was never a huge fan of buffets, but I had come to appreciate the one at the Four Feathers. The food was quite good, and the servers kept the food fresh.

Normally, a buffet didn't allow takeout, but Ruby Mae's relatives rarely permitted us to leave without containers. To avoid questions, the servers packed containers. Sometimes, Ruby Mae notified them whenever we were leaving, and they'd make sure the bags were taken to the coat check. Or I would take bags to the car so we wouldn't have to carry them around the casino with us. Tonight, we had mostly desserts, so when we were done eating, I got my exercise taking bags to the car before I came back to play.

Irma rarely played more than twenty dollars and then went to the bar to pick up men. Ruby Mae played about the same and then sat in front of the massive fireplaces that flanked the front entrance and talked to her family and friends. Nana Jo played poker, while Dorothy usually played blackjack in the high-roller room. On a day when I felt lucky, I'd splurge and play fifty dollars, which went a long way when you were playing penny slots.

Today, I wasn't feeling particularly lucky, so I meandered around the room. I saw Ruby Mae knitting near the fireplace. For once, she was alone, so I decided to sit and have a talk.

A ball of navy blue yarn fell off her lap and rolled down the hall, and I stopped to pick it up.

"I love this color. What are you making?"

Ruby Mae smiled and held out a rectangular panel that looked like a baby blanket. "What do you see?"

"Um, I see navy and yellow stripes." I frowned. "Is this one of those tests where you tell me this ball of yarn isn't really navy but pink?"

"Not at all." She stood up and held the panel in front of her at an angle, so I looked at the panel from the side. "Now what do you see?"

I narrowed my gaze and stared at the panel. In a few moments, what I thought were only yellow stripes revealed a picture. It was the famous Vermeer painting, *Girl with a Pearl Earring*. "Oh my God! How in the world did you do that?" I blinked several times, but the painting was still there as long as I didn't look head-on.

She sat down. "It's called illusion knitting."

"But how in the world did you do it? This is the most amazing thing I've ever seen."

She smiled. "Actually, it's not hard. It's just the two basic stitches, knit and purl. I don't fully understand the math, but I went to a workshop at Ivelyse's Yarn Shop a few months ago about coded knitting."

"What's that?"

"I had no idea that people have been using codes in quilts and knitting since . . . well, for thousands of years. The teacher was a wonderful woman named Patricia Lillie. She called it steganography. Did you know in World War One, Belgium women would look out their windows and either purl when they saw a German artillery train or drop a stitch, which left a hole? The Red Cross allowed soldiers of war to receive the items. The soldiers would count the purls or dropped stitches and figure out German troop movements."

"That's fascinating. I think I've read about that somewhere, but I've never seen it."

Ruby Mae nodded and continued to knit. "Most women were just knitting socks or sweaters for troops. However, some women deliberately spied and passed along information that helped win the war. She said the practice continued in the second world war and probably is still being used today." She smiled. "I like that women, even an old woman like me, could do something to help."

Ruby Mae and I talked for a few moments until one of her great-nieces came out to spend her break with her great-aunt. I decided to leave them alone and wandered off in search of a slot machine.

I sat down at a machine with a golden buffalo charging on the front. I'd played the game before and knew that it wouldn't require a great deal of thought on my part. The more buffa-loes that appeared on the screen, the better.

I put my twenty dollars in the machine and pressed "play."

I thought about Martha Chiswick and her husband. I was relieved at the thought that someone else was getting the police's attention. Detectives Deevers and Fieldstone had latched onto me as their prime suspect in the murder, and I hoped that Martha Chiswick's attempts to flee would help them realize that other people had a reason to kill Delia Marshall. In fact, there were a lot of people who might have wanted to kill Delia. She had been blackmailing Evelyn Randolph and threatened to tell her husband where she was hiding. She also trashed Evelyn and Martha's book. I'd read a story about an author who stalked a reviewer who left a bad review, and that review hadn't appeared in newspapers across the world.

Delia was blackmailing Denver Benedict. If word got out that he'd lied about the articles that cemented his career as a writer, his reputation would have suffered, especially now that he's trying to raise money for a play. Did Denver Benedict kill Delia to prevent her from telling his secret?

Martha Chiswick was a bigamist. I wonder if her husband knew? Wouldn't the information about Martha have come to light during the vetting process for him to become a judge? Would it matter? Technically, Ethan Chiswick wasn't guilty of a crime. Was he? I'd have to ask Jenna. Regardless, the embarrassment would be enough for Martha to want Delia dead.

But were any of them the big fish that Delia thought she'd landed? Delia was going to meet someone the night she was murdered. Who? What did she have on them? Was the answer in her journal? If not, why bother putting it in code?

I had more questions than answers, and the buffaloes had not been kind. I glanced at my machine and saw that I was down to sixty cents. I pressed "play" and gathered my purse to leave. That's when all of the buffaloes decided to show up. With that one spin, my sixty cents turned into five hundred dollars. I cashed out.

The casino had a hotel that was a lot quieter. I found a seat near a large plant and pulled out my laptop.

Lady Clara Trewellen-Harper sat on a high-backed sofa in the drawing room of Brown's Hotel on Dover Street. The mahogany-paneled walls gave the hotel a masculine feel that contrasted with overstuffed floral print chairs, pillows, and drapes. Despite the hotel's old-fashioned air, Lady Clara enjoyed Brown's. Whenever she could afford it, she loved to come for tea.

Lady Clara glanced around the room as she waited for her friend. The clientele of Brown's Hotel was middle-aged. An older American couple sitting near the fireplace kept remarking on the "quaint" hotel where Mark Twain was rumored to have stayed, even though Brown's staff were the soul of discretion and never revealed any information about the hotel's famous and distinguished guests. Lady Clara recognized two dukes and a member of Parliament in a corner. However, her attention was drawn to the only other young person, a cleric sitting nearby with books and journals strewn across the entire surface of the table. The scholarly looking young man had curly brown hair and spectacles. He was absorbed in his books but would periodically scribble furiously in a leather-bound journal.

"Clara!" Claire Hollingsworth rushed to her old friend and gave her a warm hug.

"Claire, I'm so glad you were able to meet with me." Lady Clara filled her own cup and then poured tea for her friend. "My goodness, you haven't aged a day."

Claire Hollingsworth was tall and slender with intelligent eyes and thick brown hair. She wasn't the type of woman men would look at twice, but she had a keen wit and a sharp mind that men found intriguing.

"You always were a good liar but thank you." She peered over her cup at her friend and smiled. "You've got a glow that only a woman in love can have."

"Does it show?" Lady Clara sipped her tea.

"What duke, baron, or landed gentleman has managed to capture the heart of Lady Clara Trewellen-Harper?"

"None of the above. I've fallen in love with a common, everyday copper." Lady Clara chuckled. "And I intend to marry him and learn to cook and clean and darn socks and knit jumpers and make a fantastic wife." She sighed. "That is if I can ever convince him that having a title doesn't mean two beans, especially if you don't have the money that goes along with the title."

"Aww. One of those?"

"Afraid so." Lady Clara took a deep breath. "But I am determined." She took a bite of her sandwich and frowned. "I don't know who came up with the idea to put watercress on bread, but they should have been locked up in the Tower." She pushed the triangle away and bit into a pastry that was oozing with lemon curd. "Now, are you really going to run for Parliament?"

Claire shrugged. "I've been asked to fight for the seat in Melton for the Labor Party, but I don't know. Everything is so uncertain right now."

Something in her voice made Lady Clara ask, "War?"

"If Britain goes to war, and it seems highly likely that we will, then I want to do my part. I want to help."

The two women talked of serious things for several minutes, but then Claire glanced at her watch. "I have to get back to work, and as much as I'd like to believe that you invited me to tea just to catch up on old times, I know you better than that. What's going on?"

"Did you know Milicent Schmidt?"

"I did, and I didn't like her. She was the worst type of journalist. Only interested in salacious stories. It's hard enough for women journalists to be taken seriously without women like her who don't care about the facts and are willing to listen at keyholes and report rumors that serve no useful purpose other than to ruin lives."

"Did she blackmail or extort money?" Lady Clara asked.

"I heard rumors that she wasn't above it. She had an expensive flat here in Mayfair, and I can attest to the fact that the *London Times* doesn't pay lady journalists enough to live in this neighborhood." She paused. "Rumor is that Millie would assume that everyone had a secret they didn't want to get out. She'd pretend like she knew something and then trick the person into spilling the beans. If that didn't work, then she'd get them to pay her to keep it secret. The thing is, she didn't know anything. They should have told her to go to the devil. That's what I would have done if she'd tried that with me."

"She sounds like a horrible person," Lady Clara said.

"Men liked her, but that's about all I know. Does that help?"

"I'm not sure, but I do appreciate the information. If you think of anything else, give me a ring." Lady Clara passed a card to her friend.

Claire Hollingsworth grabbed a scone and hurried out.

Lady Clara sat for several minutes thinking. She was startled when the cleric suddenly yelled, "Eureka!"

He blushed with embarrassment when he realized what he'd done. He gave a shy smile and leaned toward Lady Clara and said, "I'm terribly sorry. I just made a major breakthrough, and I allowed my emotions to get the better of me."

She smiled. "It's quite all right. Congratulations on your breakthrough."

"It's really rather fascinating. I've been deciphering hieroglyphs from ancient Egypt, and I finally figured out something that had been bothering me. I feel absolutely giddy. I think I know how Jean-François Champollion must have felt when he finally deciphered the Rosetta Stone."

Lady Clara glanced from the man to the books. "I'm afraid I don't know much about Egyptian hieroglyphs . . . well, nothing actually. But would you mind sharing what you figured out and how?"

The man's face lit up. He slid closer and brought two of his books.

The majority of the conversation went over Lady Clara's head, but she was fascinated by how the

Rosetta Stone was used as a key to unlock the ancient symbols.

After a quarter of an hour, the man finally stopped talking and sat up. "I'm terribly sorry. I must be boring you to tears. I—"

"Actually, I think you've just helped me solve a puzzle that's been bothering me. So, thank you." Lady Clara smiled and gathered her things. She needed to get back to Windsor Castle.

Lord James Browning returned to Windsor Castle just after dark. Standing outside smoking, he noticed a shadow skulking along the castle wall. The duke was suspicious and followed the shadow, careful to remain hidden.

The shadow made its way away from the castle, and the duke was unable to tell if he was following a man or a woman until the shadow was caught in the headlights of a passing car. That was when he realized that he had been following Lady Lucille Redding, the queen's lady-in-waiting.

James followed Lady Redding to an inn down a backstreet in the village. Lady Redding glanced around furtively before sneaking into a side entrance. While the duke debated with himself about pursuing her, he saw another shadowy figure. He backed up against the wall, out of sight. The figure followed the same path that Lady Redding had taken moments earlier. Unlike when Lady Redding passed, no cars illuminated the face of her pursuer, but Lord Browning was sure he knew who it was.

The pursuer entered the inn, and Lord Browning quickly followed. He caught sight of the man's coat as he climbed to the third floor of the inn. He knocked once, paused. Knocked twice and paused. Then knocked three times. After the third knock, the door was opened, and the figure slipped inside.

Just before the door latched, Lord Browning pushed his way inside.

He found Lady Lucille Redding clasped in an embrace with her paramour, Clive Elliott, the king's private secretary.

Chapter 20

"Eureka!" I lifted both arms in the air as if I'd just scored a touchdown. Thankfully, very few people were hanging around the casino's hotel lobby.

I saved my work, collected my things, and hurried downstairs. I couldn't wait to share my newly formed idea with Nana Jo and the girls.

Everyone was waiting in the lobby by the time I arrived.

"It's the book," I blurted out. "It's a cipher key."

"What on earth are you talking about?" Nana Jo asked. "What's a cipher key?"

"It's . . . well, it's a key." I searched for the right words but couldn't find them.

"Let's settle up, and then you can get the car. Hopefully, by then, you can explain to us what a cipher key is."

By "settling up," Nana Jo meant dividing our winnings. When Nana Jo and the girls started going to the casino, they agreed they would share all of their winnings at the end of the night. When I started coming to the casino with them, they insisted that I join the group. *All for One and One for All.* My win on the buffalo slot machine was pretty good, and all in all,

I went home with eight hundred dollars more than I'd left with. Not bad for a twenty-dollar investment.

I brought the car around, and Nana Jo and the girls all piled in.

"Now, what exactly did you decipher?" Nana Jo asked.

I explained that I thought the key to figuring out Delia Marshall's journal was the Agatha Christie books. "That's why her library record had so many Agatha Christie books. I'll bet she used those books as the key to deciphering her code."

"I don't understand," Dorothy said. "How?"

"Well, I haven't figured out the exact code yet. But I feel sure that's why she had so many Agatha Christie books, and that's why she was willing to spend over a thousand dollars to get that book custom made in England." I drove and glanced in the rearview mirror at my passengers.

We talked about the journal and how cipher keys worked for the remainder of the trip back to Shady Acres. Everyone had photos from the journal, so I suggested they take a look at those pages as well as pages from Agatha Christie's books to see if anyone noticed a pattern.

"Sort of like a cryptogram?" Ruby Mae asked.

"Sort of. I'm not sure what type of pattern she used, but remember what we talked about. Single letters are probably *A* or *I*. I think if you look for patterns, maybe we can figure out how to decrypt it."

Everyone was excited and eager to get started and promised to give it a good shot before tomorrow's meeting.

As soon as I got home, I pulled out every Agatha Christie book I owned, which was pretty much all of her mysteries and short stories. I didn't have the plays or works she'd written under her Mary Westmacott pseudonym, but I prayed Delia would have stuck to the mysteries. Nana Jo sent the pictures to the wireless printer, and we sat at the kitchen table and tried to decipher Delia Marshall's journal.

I was confident that I was right about Agatha Christie being the key. However, having the key and knowing how to use it are two different things. Nana Jo and I stared at those photos for so long I could see numbers when I closed my eyes.

"I've looked at those numbers so long, I'm getting cross-eyed," Nana Jo said. "I'm going to bed." She stood up and stretched. "I suggest you do the same. Your brain is tired. You need a good night's sleep."

I knew she was right, but I wasn't willing to give up quite so easily. I sat up staring at those pages so long that the numeric string became etched on my brain. Around three in the morning, I decided to try reading the Christie novels instead, in the hopes that something would leap off the page and suddenly everything would make sense. It didn't.

"Sam, wake up!" Nana Jo shook my arm.

For a split second, I went back in time to one week earlier when the tornado touched down in North Harbor. That was the moment that started my most recent nightmare. It's also the moment when lightning struck, and I figured out the cipher.

I pulled out my envelope with the list of books that Delia checked out from the library. The first book was *The Mysterious Affair at Styles*. There was a date at the top of each page. I looked on the envelope, and there was a book checked out on each of the dates. I flipped through the pages until I found the one that coincided with the date she checked out *Styles*.

I was excited and took several deep breaths to calm myself down. Then I glanced over the sheet and looked for a good place to start.

There was a series of three numbers. I'd read so much about ciphers that I thought it would be safe to assume that the first number would either be the page or line number. That's when I stopped.

Nana Jo was back. "You've got that look in your eyes. You've figured it out, haven't you?"

"Maybe . . . I'm not sure. I think she must have used an Ottendorf cipher."

"What on earth is that?"

"It's a cipher attributed to Major Nicholas Dietrich, Baron de Ottendorf. He was a German mercenary who was commissioned by the Continental Congress back in 1776. I don't know if Major Dietrich created the cipher, but . . . it basically uses pages, lines, and words in a book, like say . . . the Bible, to send coded messages."

Nana Jo scooted closer. "How does that help us?"

"If I'm right, and Agatha Christie is the key, then I should be able to pull up my copy of one of her books and figure out the code, but . . . I'm not sure."

"Well, let's give it a try. How can I help?"

I explained my theory about the dates on the top of the journal pages aligning to the books she checked out of the library.

"Makes sense, but how can you be sure that the pages are the same? I mean, page five hundred in my Bible isn't the same as page five hundred in your Bible."

"I think that's why Delia was so particular about the book she custom ordered from me. As long as the books are the same edition from the same publisher, I think we're golden." I crossed my fingers.

"How can I help?"

I handed Nana Jo the journal pages. "You read the numbers, and I'll look them up and jot down what we come up with."

Nana Jo rattled off numbers for five minutes, while I looked them up in the Christie book and wrote down the answers. It was a slow process, but eventually I had enough letters, and the letters spelled D-E-N-V-E-R B-E-N-E-D-I-C-T.

"That's great, but at this rate, it's going to take a long time to decipher all of these," Nana Jo said.

"I know, and without the exact same edition of the books, no one else can help."

"Why do you suppose she went to all of this trouble?" Nana Jo asked. "I mean, she could have typed it into her laptop and password protected the file if she was afraid someone would figure out what she was doing."

I shrugged. "No idea, but let's finish this one. Maybe we'll know more once we decipher one."

It took over an hour to decipher one page. When we were done, we knew what Delia had on Denver Benedict and that he had paid over twenty thousand dollars into a secret bank account.

"Do you think we should give this to Detectives Deevers and Fieldstone?" I asked.

"Why? They have the original journal. Plus, they have their own forensic geeks who should be able to decipher the code just like you did." Nana Jo was obviously still bitter.

"True. Plus, they have Delia's custom-ordered book, which is the exact edition they need to decode her journal, but I'm sure they haven't figured out to use the Agatha Christie book as a key."

Nana Jo was unusually silent, which told me she was holding something back.

"What?" I asked.

She took a deep breath. "I think we will *eventually* need to take this to the police, but I think we need to figure out what she wrote about you, just in case. . . ."

"Good point. What if Delia didn't have time to put her latest remarks, her change of heart in suing me, in the journal?"

Nana Jo nodded.

"Maybe we should skip to the end." I flipped through the pages until I found the last entry.

It only took one line on the last page to realize that Nana Jo was right. The name on the top of the page was mine.

Chapter 21

"Well, dadgummit!" Nana Jo slapped her hand on the table.

"Maybe she didn't have time to add her latest victim?" I said.

"Good thing we didn't notify Detectives Deevers and Fieldstone."

I bit my lip.

"What? Don't tell me you're going to tell those two what you found?" The disbelief was etched across her face.

"I don't want to hide or withhold information from the police. I'm in enough trouble as it is."

We discussed next steps, and I agreed that I would wait until I decoded all of the pages just in case there was something that would help find Delia's killer. I also agreed to run everything by Jenna before calling the police.

Nana Jo whipped out her cell phone and sent a text message notifying everyone that we would move our meeting to the evening. When she finished, she stared at me. "You look like death warmed over. Why not take a nap? This will go a lot faster if your mind is fresh."

As much as I wanted to get this over with, I realized that

my reflexes were slower, and I was getting the beginnings of a headache. "Okay, I'll take a one-hour nap, and then I'll get up, and we'll finish decoding."

Nana Jo agreed. "I'll set an alarm with *She Who Must Not Be Named.*"

With that promise, I headed into my bedroom, followed by my poodle entourage.

I didn't expect that I would sleep, but I must have been more exhausted than I realized because I was knocked out as soon as my head hit the pillow. I awoke with a start, just thirty minutes later. I felt as though I'd slept through the night, even though it had been little more than a power nap. I couldn't remember what I dreamed about while I slept, but I awoke with an idea floating around the back of my head. Sadly, whenever I reached out to grab it, it drifted further and further away.

Instead of chasing it, I decided to spend my remaining time in the British countryside.

In the king's drawing room, Lady Elizabeth sat by the fire and knitted while she waited for the rest of her family to arrive for their meeting. Lady Elizabeth smiled at the thought that this was her family. Some were family by blood, others by marriage, and Thompkins and Detective Inspector Covington were family because of the love and affection they shared.

King George, Bertie, was family, too. He was her cousin, and she had known him her entire life. And she loved and trusted him. He was an honorable man. She couldn't say that he would never kill. He'd served in the military. Given the right circumstances, he would do what had to be done. However, she knew he wouldn't kill someone simply to hide a secret. Bertie had never wanted to be king. He hadn't been raised for the role. No, that responsibility fell to his brother David. He should have been the one wearing the crown and shouldering the burdens of the empire.

Lady Elizabeth stopped to count her stitches. She'd inadvertently dropped a stitch and took a few moments to correct her mistake. When she had that straightened out, she allowed her mind to wander.

Lady Elizabeth allowed her mind to play the game of *What-If*. What if David hadn't abdicated the throne to marry Wallis Simpson? What if Milicent Schmidt had confronted David with her accusations? Could she imagine David murdering someone? She didn't want to admit that she could.

"That's enough of that." She shook herself to get rid of the image.

Lady Elizabeth dropped another stitch. She stared at the blanket. Normally, knitting didn't require her full attention, but this time she was struggling to keep her focus. She looked at the blanket and realized she had dropped several stitches. Something about those dropped stitches triggered a thought. She pulled the scrap of lace from her bag and placed it on the table. For the first time, she examined the scrap closely.

"This is odd," she said under her breath. "There are knots. It looks like whoever knitted this didn't know what they were doing. It's almost as if—"

The door swung open, and Rivka ran in and hurled herself into Lady Elizabeth's lap.

Rivka was three with dark curly hair, dark eyes,

and rosy cheeks. She had arrived in England nearly a year ago on the Kindertransport from Poland, along with her two older brothers and several hundred other Jewish children, seeking safety in England from the Nazis.

Lady Elizabeth smiled. "Rivka, you shouldn't run inside."

Rivka's and her two brothers' parents were killed in Poland. The children were staying with their grandfather in Berlin before being placed on the ship to come to England. At only three years old, Rivka's English wasn't very good, and Lady Elizabeth's Polish was nonexistent and her German was only slightly better. Still, with a great deal of kindness, they managed to communicate quite well.

Joseph Mueller, Thompkins's son-in-law, hurried into the drawing room. "I'm terribly sorry, Lady Elizabeth. She got away from me." He frowned at Rivka and then spoke in German.

Rivka frowned and turned to Lady Elizabeth. "I'm sorry," she said slowly.

Lady Elizabeth drew the girl close. "It's okay, dear."

Rivka picked up the scrap of lace and stared. After a few moments, she turned to Lady Elizabeth and said something in German.

Lady Elizabeth looked to Joseph for an interpretation.

He frowned. "She wants to know if you were counting trains."

"Counting trains? I don't understand." Lady Elizabeth gazed from the small child to the scrap of lace. After a few seconds, her face lit up, and she pulled the child close and squeezed her. "Rivka, you're brilliant. Thank you. I think you deserve a biscuit." She looked up at Joseph. "Would you please see that Rivka gets a special treat?"

Rivka's English left much to be desired, but she understood "biscuit." She beamed and hurried over to Joseph, took his hand, and skipped out of the room.

Lady Clara Trewellen-Harper was the first to arrive. She burst into the drawing room, rushed to the table, and picked up the scrap of lace. "I thought so." She turned to Lady Elizabeth. "Do you know what this is?"

Lady Elizabeth was unraveling her blanket and rewinding the yarn onto the ball. She nodded. "If I had to guess, I'd say Morse code."

Lady Clara stared at her cousin in shock. "You've already figured it out."

She smiled. "Actually, Rivka did."

By the time the others arrived, Lady Elizabeth and Lady Clara had deciphered the shawl. They had an idea why Milicent Schmidt was murdered, but there were still quite a few loose ends that needed to be wrapped up before they had their killer.

Lord Browning offered to go first. He shared what he'd learned from Colonel Edge. He also told the group about following Lady Redding and Clive Elliott. "Lady Redding and Clive Elliott both claim their only crime is being in love."

"Cousin Lucille in love?" Lady Daphne said. "Who would have thought?"

"They say there's someone for everyone," Lady Penelope said. "I'm rather glad she's found her true love."

"If there's nothing sinister about it, then why were they hiding?" Detective Inspector Covington asked.

"The rules about fraternization within the court are very strict," Lady Elizabeth said.

Lord William sat in a chair near the fireplace, smoking his pipe. "Sir Walter Raleigh and Elizabeth Throckmorton were sent to the Tower when Queen Elizabeth discovered they'd gotten married in secret without royal permission." He chuckled. "Couldn't get away with that today."

Lady Clara stamped her foot and huffed. "Bloody invasive if you ask me."

Lord Browning hid a smile. "Certainly an archaic practice. Neither of them were in danger of imprisonment. Nevertheless, they claim they were both concerned for their positions."

"I take it Milicent Schmidt found out and threatened to tell the king?" Lady Daphne said.

Lord Browning nodded. "If the relationship was made public, they both could have been sacked, although who knows how the king would have responded. Anyway, according to Lady Redding, she pleaded with Milicent not to tell anyone."

"Based on what I learned about Milicent Schmidt today, I can only imagine how she responded to that," Lady Clara said.

Lord Browning filled his pipe. "She laughed, according to Lady Redding."

"Who else knew about their relationship?" Lady Elizabeth said. She stopped winding yarn and looked up. "I find it hard to believe they didn't have help."

Thompkins gave a soft discreet cough from the corner where he stood and said, "The servants knew."

Lady Penelope hopped up from her seat, crossed her arms, and paced. "Alice Jamison knew." She huffed. "While Victor and Lieutenant Jamison were talking about military stuff, Alice let slip that she found out about Lady Redding and Clive Elliott. She said she thought it was romantic."

Something in Lady Penelope's manner made Lady Elizabeth ask, "But you don't believe her?"

Lady Penelope took a few more turns in front of the fireplace before she stopped pacing and faced the group. "It's not that I don't believe her. I believe she did help her. I guess I'm just questioning her motives."

Lady Daphne stared at her sister. "You don't like Alice?"

"No. I don't know why. She seems nice enough, but I felt like she was hiding something." Lady Penelope frowned. "There were times when I felt . . . oh, I don't know. I felt hatred."

"You can't arrest someone for a feeling," Victor said. "Just because you don't like her doesn't mean she's a murderer." He sat in front of the fireplace and gazed at his wife.

"I know, but there's something wrong. I just can't put my finger on it." Lady Penelope paced. "Plus, there's that German, Herbert von Dirksen, she invited to lunch."

"We're going to have to be cautious," Lady Elizabeth said. "Every German isn't a Nazi. If we aren't careful, we'll find ourselves filled with the same hatred and intolerance."

Lord Browning rose from his seat. "True, but we also have to be vigilant. England is very probably going to be at war, and we don't know who we can trust."

"Do you believe Schmidt really knew something about the sinking of HMS *Thetis*?" Victor asked.

"Colonel Edge's story matches perfectly what Lieutenant Jamison told me. I've known Jamison for years, and I don't think he'd lie. I also don't think he'd deliberately sink a ship that cost nearly a hundred men their lives."

"Colonel Edge is an excellent judge of character," Lord Browning said, smiling. "He may not be the most proper soldier, but he's definitely a good one."

"Agreed," Victor said. "But I still can't believe that Roland Jamison is a spy."

"Perhaps Lieutenant Jamison isn't the spy," Lady Elizabeth said. "There's another option." She finished rolling her ball of yarn and turned to her cousin. "Clara, perhaps you should explain."

Lady Clara came over to the sofa where Lady Elizabeth was sitting and picked up the scrap of lace. "I thought there was something odd about this lace."

"You're not a knitter, so that would make sense," Lady Elizabeth said. "I'm ashamed to say that I couldn't figure it out either. It wasn't until Rivka came in that—"

"Rivka?" Lord William said. "She's only three years old."

"She's a smart little girl who's been through a lot in her young life," Lady Elizabeth said. "She looked at the yarn and asked if I was counting trains."

Lord Browning's eyes enlarged, and he rushed forward and gazed at the lace. "By God . . ."

"Counting trains?" Lady Daphne said. "I don't understand."

"It's Morse code," Lady Clara said. "Since I've started working at Bletchley Park, I've had to learn Morse code and all the various ways that it's been used. It wasn't until I was having tea at Brown's Hotel and noticed a cleric sitting nearby decoding ancient Egyptian hieroglyphs that I remembered."

Lord William sat forward in his seat and stared at the lace. "Well, I'll be a monkey's uncle."

Lady Daphne frowned. "I don't understand. What do ancient Egyptian hieroglyphs and Morse code have to do with the queen mother's lace shawl and counting trains?"

Lady Elizabeth smiled. "I first heard about steganography during the Great War, although I believe it's been going on for thousands of years."

"What's steganography?" Lady Penelope asked.

"Basically, it refers to hiding secret messages in ordinary items so as not to arouse suspicion," Lady Clara said.

"That's right," Lord Browning said. "It's been around for thousands of years in one form or another."

Lady Elizabeth pulled out her knitting needles and began to cast yarn as she spoke. "During the war, I was heavily involved with the Red Cross. The Geneva Conventions allowed medical supplies and aid for soldiers and prisoners of war. When the government realized there was a great opportunity to not only provide much-needed medical supplies and humanitarian aid but to also help our country, some of the women were trained in a form of Morse code."

"I heard that Belgian intelligence agents made friends with elderly women who lived near the railway," Lord Browning said. "Those with windows that overlooked the rail would monitor passing Imperial German train movements and somehow note it in their knitting." He glanced at Lady Elizabeth for confirmation.

She nodded. "Knitting is really easy. It's basically two stitches." She held up the small patch that she'd managed to knit quickly. "There's the knit stitch, which is usually the front, and a purl, which is often the back. You can make various patterns by alternating those two simple stitches or create interesting designs by dropping or increasing stitches." She flipped the item to show the back.

"Morse code is basically a series of dots and dashes," Lady Clara said. "If the knitting is the dots, then the purls could be dashes. Or vice versa."

"You can also simply drop a stitch, which will leave a hole in the pattern," Lady Elizabeth said. "So, the women would sit at their windows and knit all day and purl whenever they saw an artillery train or drop a stitch if a troop railcar passed."

A lightbulb went on, and Detective Inspector Covington's eyes lit up. "So, they could send that coded scarf to their sons on the front lines and let them know how many troop cars the enemy was sending?"

Lady Clara smiled. "Exactly."

Lord William chomped on the stem of his pipe. "Darned clever. I received scarves and socks in Red Cross packages. Never knew to check for codes."

"Not all packages were coded," Lady Elizabeth said. "Some socks and jumpers were just that. Hundreds of thousands of women sent packages during the war."

"It makes me proud to think of those brave women who were willing to risk their lives to do their bit for their countries," Lady Clara said. She dabbed at her eyes with a handkerchief slipped from her sleeve.

"They were brave," Lord Browning said. "If they had been caught, they risked imprisonment or execution."

Victor glanced at the scrap of lace. "So, the queen mother's shawl is a coded message?"

Lady Elizabeth nodded. "I'm afraid so."

"But surely you're not saying the queen mother was passing along coded messages?" Detective Inspector Covington took out a handkerchief and wiped his neck.

"Not knowingly," Lady Elizabeth said. "She received the shawl as a gift from her goddaughter. So, you see, the spy wasn't Lieutenant Jamison. It was his wife, Alice."

"But who was she passing the information to, and how did she manage to get the documents from the king's red box?" Victor asked.

"I suspect when Alice discovered that the king's personal secretary, Clive Elliott, and Lady Redding were involved, she took advantage of the situation. She pretended to be helping the couple with their secret assignations. When in actuality, she just needed to get the two of them out of the way so her accomplice could use the tunnels to sneak into the castle."

"Dear God," Victor said.

"How do we prove it?" Lord Browning asked.

Lady Elizabeth smiled. "Well, I have an idea."

Chapter 22

The alarm went off, and I was thrust back into the present. I returned to the kitchen, where I found Nana Jo sitting at the table where I'd left her.

She glanced up. "I hope you got some rest. Although I heard you moving about. I know writing helps you figure things out, so I didn't disturb you."

"I rested some, and I wrote a bit. I don't know that I figured out who murdered Delia Marshall, but it looks like you've been busy." I looked at the papers strewn across the table.

Nana Jo had continued to decipher Delia Marshall's journal. "I deciphered the pages about Denver Benedict, Evelyn Randolph, and a couple of other folks who don't live in Michigan."

"Any big revelations?"

She stretched. "Not really. I was just about to start on Martha Chiswick."

"Why don't you let me tackle that while you take a break." I sat down and pulled the Agatha Christie books closer and studied the notepad where Nana Jo had been writing.

Deciphering the Ostendorf code was slow work. Eventually I had all of the letters and just needed to assemble them to find out what Delia had written.

Nana Jo sat down. "Anything new?"

The first part of Delia's message wasn't anything new. "Delia found out Martha Chiswick got married at a very young age to Wayne Kramer. Kramer was a conman and made her life miserable. He told her he'd gotten a divorce, so when she met and fell in love with Ethan Chiswick, she thought she was free to marry. It wasn't until later that Delia learned Kramer never went through with the divorce."

"So, Delia Marshall decides to capitalize on this knowledge and blackmail her. Some friend." Nana Jo sipped her coffee. "Why didn't Martha get divorced?"

"After Ethan became a judge, Martha was probably too scared."

"Hmm. I'll bet Delia Marshall didn't help matters. She probably told her she'd notify the authorities and humiliate the judge. I don't think Martha is the brightest crayon in the box. I'd have told her to go jump off a bridge."

"Everyone doesn't have your inner strength." I replaced numbers with letters and read on. "Interesting, it looks like Preston Kincaid is Judge Chiswick's assistant."

"Kincaid? Isn't he that lawyer that Jenna told us about?"

"He is. And I think we've found Delia's next target."

"What do you mean?"

I tapped my notepad. "Delia discovered that Kincaid had written a book under a pseudonym and had just gotten a large advance, and the film rights were also being auctioned."

"I know what film rights are, but what's an auction?"

"It means when multiple companies are interested in buying the rights to make the book into a film. They go to auction, and the companies compete against each other. An auction usually results in a lot of money for the author. At least, that's how Pamela explained it to me when she was sending my manuscript out to publishers. Unfortunately, my book didn't go to auction, but it looks like Preston Kincaid's did. Remember that thesis that Delia sent away for?"

Nana Jo nodded.

"Delia suspected Kincaid stole it from a deceased friend. That's why she sent away for the manuscript."

"Some friend," she mumbled.

"Preston Kincaid has finally turned his life around. He's an aide to a judge who's about to get appointed to the state supreme court, and he has a HUGE book and film deal hanging in the balance. And Delia Marshall was about to ruin all of it."

"That sounds like a good motive for murder," Nana Jo said.

Chapter 23

"I think it's time I called the police." I picked up my phone.

"Sam, I agree you need to do something, but do you really believe Detectives Deevers and Fieldstone will listen?"

I sighed. "I'd like to believe they won't let their personal feelings interfere with their jobs."

"So would I, but this is too important to trust those two Neanderthals will do the right thing," Nana Jo said. "Call Jenna."

I picked up all of the pictures and the notepad and put everything into a shopping bag. "Better yet, I'll just head over to Jenna's house and take all of this stuff. That way, if she's still mad, she can't hang up."

I took the bag downstairs and drove to my sister's house. I was so excited. Maybe this nightmare would be over soon, and I could not only enjoy my life, but I could enjoy my book release.

I hurried up the stairs and rang the bell.

Jenna opened the door a crack, so only her face was visible. "Sam, this isn't a good time. I'm not feeling well. Could you come back later?" Jenna moved to close the door, but I stopped her.

"Jenna, wait, I figured it out. I deciphered Delia Marshall's journal. I know who killed her." I stared at my sister, who looked pale and frightened. "What's wrong? You're not still angry about what happened at the police station, are you?"

"I'm not angry, but this *really* isn't a good time." She tried to close the door again, but this time I was worried.

"Jenna, if you're sick, you shouldn't be alone. Let me in." I pushed the door open.

The door opened wider, and I could see that Jenna wasn't alone. Standing behind her was a tall man with a big gun.

"By all means, do come inside," he said.

Chapter 24

The man was tall with dark hair, glasses, and a look in his dark eyes that told me he wasn't quite sane.

Inside, he slammed the door shut and motioned with his gun for me to move into Jenna's study.

"You must be Preston Kincaid," I said.

He narrowed his gaze and stared for a few moments. "Have we met?"

Jenna and I walked slowly into the study. There were law books piled atop every flat surface.

Standing next to my sister, I whispered, "Tony?"

"He went to a lecture at MISU."

Kincaid grinned. "Oh, nobody's coming. I made sure of that."

"What do you mean by that?" Jenna asked.

"Where do you think your husband got that ticket for tonight's lecture?" He chuckled.

Jenna took a step forward, and Kincaid extended his gun. "That's enough. I've heard you're a tough litigator, but not even a pit bull can stop a bullet." He pointed at my bag. "Is that the evidence? Delia's journal?"

"The police have the journal. I just have some photos of the pages."

"Where'd you find it? I tore her apartment to pieces looking for that journal."

"So you're the one who trashed Delia's house?"

He grinned. "Who else? Delia was stupid. Blackmailers are all stupid. There are only two ways blackmail can end. Either the victim goes to the police and the blackmailer is prosecuted. Or . . ." He grinned.

"Or?" I asked.

"Or, the victim gets tired of paying out and takes matters into their own hands." He grinned again. His grin confirmed my initial impression. He wasn't sane. "The blackmail is stopped one way or the other. You can do it legally or illegally, but it can't continue forever." He paused for a beat. "Now, hand it over."

I extended the bag, and Kincaid snatched it out of my hand. He opened the bag and pulled out one of the pages and looked it over. He stared at the numbers for several seconds, but eventually shoved the page back into the bag.

"Now you can let us go. You have what you want."

He threw back his head and laughed. "You must be kidding. If I let you go, you'll just go to the police and tell them what you know. Let's not pretend that we don't know how this is going to play out . . . how it has to end. You ladies are too smart for that."

"We won't go to the police. I promise. Besides, the police probably wouldn't believe me anyway. They think I killed Delia Marshall."

"They should have accused you. She was killed in your bookshop. Plus, she was going to sue you, just like she threatened to do to me and so many others." He cocked his head to the side. "But you managed to wiggle out of the trap I set. I won't make that mistake again."

"Just out of curiosity, how did you get into my book-shop?" I asked.

"Piece of cake." He reached in his pocket and pulled out a small device that was about the size of a television remote control. "This is a jammer or 'interference generator.' Its pur-pose is to jam the signal within wireless security systems." He gazed at the device lovingly before returning it to his pocket. "Three years of law school and I'm amazed at the things you can learn working in the criminal justice system." He laughed. "Once inside, I found the security system control panel and disconnected the main and backup power supplies. I waited to make sure the alarm company didn't send someone out to check." He shrugged. "My sources tell me that immediately following a power outage, like a tornado, security companies will be short-staffed trying to get all of their equipment work-ing, so that was the ideal time to hit." He repositioned his gun at me. "Now, back to business."

"How'd you get Delia to come here? I mean, I was on the phone with her and she wanted me to come to meet her." I rushed to keep him talking.

"Delia required a bit of . . . coaxing, shall we say." He grinned. "But it's amazing how easily people will comply with a gun pointed at their heads. I mean, you two have been very cooperative and while I'd like to believe that it's because of my persuasive personality, I suspect this little baby has some-thing to do with it." He pointed his gun and smirked.

"So you planned to kill Delia from the beginning?" I asked.

"Did you miss that part where I told you there were only two ways to deal with blackmail? It wasn't likely that I was going to go to the police. So, murder was inevitable." He pointed the gun and aimed. "Now, who wants to go first?"

"Wait. You can't just shoot us," I said.

"Watch me."

"But how are you going to explain both Jenna and me getting shot?"

"You two interrupted an intruder—"

"But the gun. They'll trace the gun back to you and—"

He was shaking his head before the words were out of my mouth. "Now, you might *assume* that a criminal who doesn't want to have a gun traced back to them would just steal it, but you'd be wrong. Actually, stolen guns only account for about ten percent of guns used in crimes." He shook his head, puffed out his chest, and struck a pose that would have won an Oscar for best dramatic portrayal of a lawyer playing to a jury during a trial. "No, the number-one way that criminals get guns is through a 'straw purchase.'" He stopped and looked pointedly at me. "Do you know what that is?"

"Never heard of it," I said honestly.

"I'll bet the pit bull here knows." He glanced at Jenna.

If he knew my sister the way I know my sister, he would have recognized the signs of a volcano that's about to blow. Her gaze narrowed. Her brow furled. Her nostrils flared. And her chest heaved with each breath. Despite Kincaid's taunting, Jenna remained silent.

In that moment, I wasn't sure if I was more afraid of the killer with the gun or my sister. If there was a way out of this situation that didn't lead to bloodshed, I didn't see it.

Kincaid paused for a beat and then shrugged and continued his lecture. "Well, a straw purchase is when someone who wants to buy a gun, but wants to remain anonymous, gets someone else to make the purchase on their behalf." He paused for his words to sink in. "The second biggest way criminals get guns is to buy them from legally licensed but corrupt at-home and commercial gun dealers. And last, but certainly not least, there are unlicensed street dealers who either get their guns through illegal transactions with licensed dealers, straw purchases, or from gun thefts." He shook his head. "I tell you, it's truly amazing the things you learn when you interact with the criminal element on a regular basis. Just one more bit of useful information that means that there is no way the police will ever be able to tie me to this gun. Even if I were stupid enough to leave the gun for them to find. Which I'm not. This gun will be wiped clean, placed in a bag with several bricks, and tossed in Lake Michigan."

My heart raced and the blood pounded in my ears.

He lifted his arm and pointed his gun at my heart. "Say good-bye."

Just as he finished talking, the front door opened, and my nephews, Christopher and Zaq, entered. They slammed the door and yelled, "Hey, Mom. You here?"

"Was that Aunt Sammy's car?" Zaq called.

The twins came around the corner and entered the office, and Preston Kincaid turned to face them.

The boys stopped. Their faces were frozen, and their eyes locked onto the gun.

Suddenly, my sister's face contorted into a wild animal. She growled. With one move, she reached over to her desk and picked up a huge dictionary that I'd seen for years, *Black's Law Dictionary*. Like Serena Williams serving at Wimbledon, Jenna swung the book and connected with Preston Kincaid's head.

The stunned lawyer dropped to his knees like a sack of potatoes.

Before I realized what had happened, Jenna leaped through the air screaming and swinging. She pummeled Kincaid with each blow she landed. She hurled threats at the lawyer for daring to point a weapon at her babies.

After the initial shock, I grabbed my sister and pulled her to the corner, while Christopher and Zaq removed the gun and secured Kincaid.

Chapter 25

Later, Detectives Deevers and Fieldstone stood silently. Chief of Police Daryl Stevenson, back from Washington, D.C., had been visiting with his great-aunt when Nana Jo called to let Ruby Mae and the girls know that the case was solved. Chief Stevenson drove them all over to Jenna's house.

Frank and Nana Jo came separately, and Jenna had sent a text to her husband to come home at once.

Jenna's small office was bursting with people, but no one cared.

"You could have been killed, Counselor," Detective Deevers said. "You should leave the police work to the professionals."

Detective Fieldstone mumbled something that sounded like "Rank amateurs."

Jenna growled, and I didn't want a repeat of her earlier performance and stepped forward.

"Perhaps I can explain," I said to Chief Stevenson.

It took quite a few minutes to explain the entire story, and I could tell by the vein pulsing on the side of Detective Fieldstone's head that he wasn't happy with my retelling. However, the look that Chief Stevenson flashed his way suggested his best course of action was silence.

When I finished, Chief Stevenson turned to Jenna. "You took a pretty big chance. Are you sure you don't want to go to the hospital and just let them check you over?"

"I'm fine. Or I will be." She closed her eyes and took several deep breaths. "I don't know what happened, but when I saw that dirtbag pointing a gun at my babies, I just snapped."

Jenna's babies, Christopher and Zaq, were six foot two and well over two hundred pounds. They grinned at the thought of their mom needing to take up for them.

"Who knew Mom had a swing like that?" Christopher joked.

"You should have seen her, Dad," Zaq said. "I thought she was going to rip that guy's face off."

Tony shook his head but kept a secure arm around his wife. "Your mom's tough." He glanced around at Nana Jo. "She comes from tough stock."

"So, Preston Kincaid killed Delia Marshall?" Chief Stevenson asked.

"Yes," I said. "Delia found out he stole the manuscript he was passing off as his own. She'd already ruined his political career. Now she was threatening to ruin his second chance."

"You should have brought all of this information to us," Detective Deevers said.

"We did. I gave you Delia's journals, and you had the Agatha Christie book, the murder weapon. You had everything we had."

Detective Deevers's ears turned red.

"I have one question," I said, turning to my nephews. "What brought you both home?"

They grinned.

"Well, we didn't want to miss your book release party," Christopher said.

Zaq grinned. "Plus, we needed to do laundry."

Chapter 26

The next few days were busy. Chief Stevenson made Deevers and Fieldstone remove the crime scene tape, and Market Street Mysteries was open for business. Murder might be bad for a number of businesses, but not a mystery bookstore. Regulars in need of their mystery fix flocked inside, along with the curious who merely wanted to see where a murder had occurred. I was grateful to have my nephews, Christopher and Zaq, on hand to help out.

To my great surprise and immense pleasure, my assistant, Dawson, his girlfriend and Dorothy's granddaughter, Jillian, and Jillian's roommate, and Zaq's girlfriend, Emma Lee, all made it back in time for my book launch party.

The morning that my book was released, I awoke to the wonderful smell of bacon, coffee, and cinnamon rolls.

Nana Jo knocked and came in with a huge smile. "Congratulations, my granddaughter, the author."

I grinned. "I can hardly believe it."

"Believe it. We've got a busy day, so you better shake a leg and get ready." She patted her thigh. "Snickers and Oreo, come."

The poodles hopped off the bed and trotted after my grandmother.

I took a moment to stretch and then got up and hopped in the shower. When I was clean, dressed, and mostly awake, I followed my nose to the kitchen.

"Congratulations!" Dawson smiled and passed me a plate of bacon, eggs, and cinnamon rolls.

"I am the luckiest girl in the world that the men in my life are great cooks, but I've got to be careful, or I'm going to need a crane to get me down the stairs."

Dawson smiled. "I love baking. It's great to get to do what you love."

Nana Jo and the poodles came back upstairs, and we ate while I fielded text messages and calls from family and friends sending well wishes and congratulations.

When I finished eating, I got up to go downstairs to open the bookstore.

"Where do you think you're going?" Nana Jo asked.

"Work?"

She shook her head. "Not today. Dawson and I have it. You stay up here and finish writing. Relax. Do some wrist exercises to prepare for your book release party. You're going to have to sign a ton of autographs."

"But the party and tea aren't until four," I whined. "I'm perfectly capable of—"

"Samantha Marie Washington, I know what you're capable of doing. Now, will you just for once allow someone to do something nice for you?"

Even without the use of my full name, I knew Nana Jo meant business. "Yes, ma'am."

Nana Jo and Dawson went downstairs, and the poodles and I remained upstairs.

After fifteen minutes that felt like an hour, I decided to take advantage of Nana Jo's suggestion and write.

The morning of young Lord William Peregrin Carlston's christening, the castle was abuzz with activity. King George VI looked out the large bay window in the king's drawing room. Lord Browning, Lord Victor Carlston, Lady Clara, Detective Inspector Covington, Lady Elizabeth, Lieutenant Jamison, and his wife, Alice, awaited the christening. Colonel Sandy Edge maintained a rigid stance in the corner of the room, dressed in his formal military uniform.

Colonel Edge tugged at the collar of his shirt and whispered to Lord Browning, "You should have told me the king was going to be here."

Lord Browning grinned. "Would you have come if I had?"

"Not on your life."

"That's why I didn't tell you." Lord Browning smiled.

Lady Elizabeth coughed discreetly. "Your Majesty, I believe we can now tell you who killed Milicent Schmidt."

Alice Jamison clutched the pearl necklace around her neck. "Oh dear, have you really figured it out?"

"Yes, we have," Lady Elizabeth said.

King George VI turned and gave a slight nod to his cousin. "Pl-please continue."

Lady Elizabeth relayed the information uncovered about Milicent Schmidt's tactics and about Lady Redding and Clive Elliott.

The king frowned. "I was afraid Elliott might be involved. He was the only one who could have g-g-gotten into that red b-b-box."

"That's the way it was meant to look, of course," Lady Elizabeth said.

"You mean he wasn't?"

"No. His only crime was falling in love, confiding in the wrong people, and trying to keep his relationship secret."

"I su-suppose in light of recent events with David, he pr-probably thought he didn't st-stand a chance." King George frowned. "The bloody fool."

Lady Elizabeth nodded to Lord Browning to continue.

"Milicent Schmidt believed every person had a secret they didn't want uncovered. She used her scare tactics to try to convince you, the queen mother, and Lieutenant Jamison here to either pay her money or reveal their secrets. She inadvertently latched onto a secret that someone was willing to kill for, but it wasn't the secret she thought it was."

"What do you mean?" the king asked.

"When Clive Elliott and Lady Redding snuck out of the castle for their secret rendezvous, Milicent Schmidt saw them. She also saw the people who helped them." Lord Browning glanced at Alice Jamison.

She smiled. "I see I've been found out." She sat up straight. "Guilty as charged. I've always been rather a romantic, and I have to say, I just couldn't help but do what I could for the lovers."

"That's not all you did," Lord Browning said. "You see, Milicent Schmidt tried to blackmail you. She saw you with a member of the German Embassy, Herbert von Dirksen. She thought your relationship was romantic."

Alice flushed. "I don't know what you're implying,

but there's absolutely nothing between Herbert von Dirksen and me."

Lieutenant Jamison stared from Lord Browning to his wife in shock. "How dare you." He stood to rise but was pushed down by Colonel Edge, who had silently slipped behind his chair.

"I dare because it's true," Lord Browning said. "She did see you with him, but she thought it was romantic. She didn't realize that there was something more sinister going on."

The color left Alice's face, and she stared open-mouthed and shocked.

"What are you talking about?" Lieutenant Jamison asked.

Victor walked over to his friend. "I'm sorry to say it's all true. Your wife, with the aid of Herbert von Dirksen, has been conspiring to steal secret documents and pass the information to Germany."

Alice stood. "Well, I never. This is ridiculous."

Lady Elizabeth pulled out her knitting. "Actually, it was quite clever. You pretended to be helping Clive Elliott when you were helping yourself to the contents of the king's red box. When Clive and Lady Redding wanted a private tryst, they phoned you. Dirksen leased an apartment at an inn near the castle. You met them at the tunnel, supposedly to help them escape, when in reality, you were using the opportunity to allow Dirksen into the castle through those same tunnels."

Lord Browning continued. "Elliott said you always left a bottle of wine for the pair. Undoubtedly drugged. Then, either you or Dirksen took the secretary's key from his coat. Dirksen then entered the castle, took pictures of the documents, and then returned the key to Elliott upon his return."

"That's absurd," Alice said.

"You traveled with the royal family when they toured Britain's Royal Naval College," Lady Clara said. "That must have been when you realized that the royal family had access to secure military installments. And you and Dirksen decided to figure out a way to get that information to Germany."

"Ridiculous." Alice turned to her husband. "Roland, are you going to listen to this nonsense?"

Lieutenant Jamison gazed from his friend to his wife in astonishment. "You're sure?"

Victor nodded.

"It's rubbish," Alice said. "Well, I'm not going to stand here and take this. I'm going—"

Colonel Sandy Edge stepped out and blocked her path. "Ma'am, I don't want to hurt a woman, so please don't make me."

"Is that when you got the idea to knit the information into a shawl using Morse code?" Lady Elizabeth asked. "Ingenious. You might have gotten away with it if the queen mother hadn't taken a fancy to the shawl and taken it."

"When Milicent Schmidt approached you, and she had that scrap of lace in her hands, you must have been frightened," Lady Clara said. "Which one of you killed her? You or Dirksen?"

Alice walked over to the window where the king was standing. She turned her back, reached into her purse, and pulled out a gun. When Lord Browning took a step forward, she turned the gun and pointed it straight at the king's head. "You're all very clever, but I intend to get out of here. Now, move back, or

Britain will be looking for yet another monarch very shortly."

She slowly walked toward the door, careful to keep the king between her and the soldiers. When she reached the door to the drawing room, she turned to grab the knob.

Detective Inspector Covington grabbed a paperweight from the king's desk and hurled it at Alice, knocking the gun from her hand.

Lord Browning pushed the king aside, while Lady Clara grabbed Alice and pinned her down.

Colonel Edge turned to Lord Browning. "You Brits really know how to hold a christening."

Later, surrounded by family and close friends, young Lord William Carlston's christening went off without a hitch. In gratitude for saving his life, King George VI knighted Detective Inspector Covington.

Afterward, Sir Peter Covington pulled Lady Clara outside to the terrace. Once the couple was outside, he quickly got down on one knee. "Lady Clara Trewellen-Harper, will you marry me?"

Lady Clara agreed.

Sir Peter pulled her close, and the two shared a passionate kiss. When they came up for air, Lady Clara snuggled close. "I would have said yes even without the title."

"I know you would." He kissed her. "And I would have proposed to you without the title, too. I love you, Lady Clara Elizabeth Trewellen-Harper."

When I finally went downstairs, the bookstore was packed. There were balloons, cake, and boxes upon boxes of books. In the conference room, there was tea, sandwiches, scones, pastries, and a large cake with the cover of my book, *Murder at Wickfield Lodge*, printed on top.

One of the biggest surprises was when I glanced up and saw my mother and Harold Robertson. I rushed over and hugged them both.

"I can't believe you came all the way from Australia for my book release." I wiped away a tear with my hand before Frank handed me a handkerchief.

"I wouldn't miss your big day for anything," my mom said.

Harold smiled and gave me a hug. "Gracie said she wished she could be here, and I knew I just had to make that happen."

Harold was a big man with a big heart. His sole desire seemed to be to make my mom happy. And that made me happy.

Nana Jo pushed her way through the crowd. She put her fingers in her mouth and whistled like she was hailing a taxi in New York City. "Listen up. I've been waiting all day to share this." She held up her iPad. "*Murder at Wickfield Lodge* got a starred review and is a number one bestseller on two different lists."

I squeezed Frank's hand. "I think I'm going to pass out."

He grinned. "Do you need mouth-to-mouth resuscitation?"

I turned and hugged him tightly. "I can't believe this is happening."

I took a deep breath and looked around at the faces of my family and friends.

"Speech!" the crowd yelled.

Frank squeezed my hand, transferring his strength to me. "I know as a writer, I should have the right words, but I don't. I don't have the words to say how much any of this means. Thank you all for coming out and for supporting me."

I sold out and took orders for more. The food was delicious. And by the end of the night, I was exhausted from crying and laughing and my cheeks hurt from smiling.

When everyone had gone home, I locked the doors and walked around the store. I turned out the lights and looked around. A wave of emotion hit me when I realized that here, tonight, both of my dreams became a reality. I not only owned the mystery bookshop that Leon and I used to dream we'd have, but I was now a published author. For a brief moment, I felt panic. *What do I do now?* However, the panic was short-lived. I thought of Frank, Nana Jo, and the girls, and I knew the answer.

I picked up Snickers and Oreo and hugged them tightly. "It's time to get a new dream."

Acknowledgments

I didn't think this book would happen and it wouldn't have if it weren't for my amazing agent, Jessica Faust at Book-Ends Literary Agency. Of course, I have to thank my editor, John Scognamiglio, for allowing me to continue Sam and Nana Jo's story. And thanks to Michelle, Carly, and all of the wonderful people at Kensington.

I've been so fortunate to have a great team of people who help me in so many different ways. Thanks to my freelance editor, Michael Dell, for always being so flexible. You're the best. Thanks to my personal assistant, Kelly Fowler, for giving me the one thing I need most, time.

Writing always involves a great deal of research. Most of it is online, but sometimes, you just need to talk to an expert. That's where Victoria Gilbert, Abby Vandiver, Debra H. Goldstein, and Alexia Gordon come in. You guys are amazing.

As always, none of this would be possible without the love, support, and encouragement of my family and friends.